CH0097219G

"Nancy Lemann has taken th
ers and returned it to a clutch.
know how to give decadence a good name. . . . 11 u.. ...
cent City should find itself in the grip of a population explo-
sion, they can blame Nancy Lemann for making her readers
want to move there. I want to have a drink at that Lafayette
Hotel."
  —Florence King, *Los Angeles Times Book Review*

"A modern Fitzgerald is launched. . . . Lemann's style can
manage succinctness, wit, and pathos all in the same sentence."
  —*Cleveland Plain Dealer*

"Striking. . . . richly rewarding. . . . Reminiscent of the works
of Eudora Welty and the late Tennessee Williams."
  —*Booklist*

"Brilliant. . . . Party scenes worthy of Evelyn Waugh . . . and a
very funny portrait of a people and place that haven't
changed, much, since the Civil War."
  —*Kirkus Reviews*

"A tremendous first novel . . . with the mysterious subtlety of
great writing."
  —*Vogue*

"Think of *Lives of the Saints* as a long poem—a hysterically
funny poem that is also beautifully written. . . . Words are
slung about recklessly, piled in staggering heaps, and what
emerges from them is an almost hypnotic portrait of unforget-
table people in a strange and magnificent city. . . . Warming
and endearing, brilliant."
  —Ann Tyler, *The New Republic*

"The author's not inconsiderable feat is the creation of a world that is simultaneously wry, absurd and moving. . . . A formidable debut performance from a novelist of exceptional gifts."

—Boston Globe

"Witty, memorable, and original. . . . Louise's tale of decency and self-destruction is poignant, serious, subtle. *Lives of the Saints,* in its flow of observations and feelings, is a superb portrait of a people whose day is not yet done."

—Vanity Fair

VOICES OF THE SOUTH

LIVES OF THE SAINTS

OTHER BOOKS BY NANCY LEMANN

The Ritz of the Bayou
Sportsman's Paradise

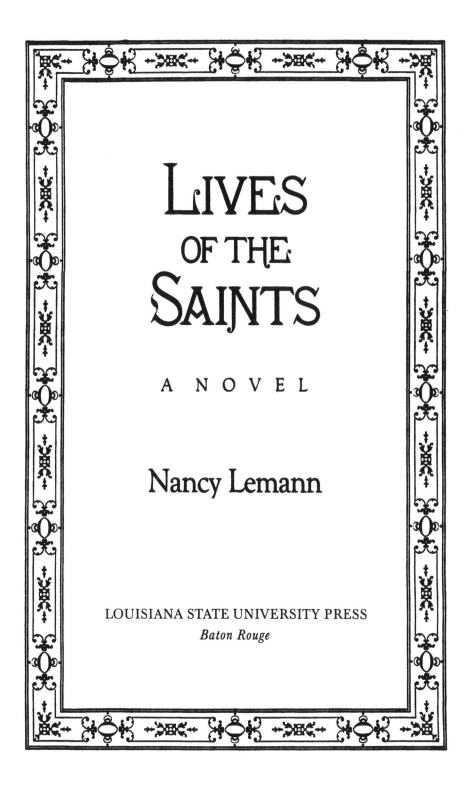

LIVES
OF THE
SAINTS

A NOVEL

Nancy Lemann

LOUISIANA STATE UNIVERSITY PRESS
Baton Rouge

Copyright © 1985 by Nancy Lemann
Originally published by Alfred A. Knopf, Inc.
LSU Press edition published 1997 by arrangement with the author.
All rights reserved
Manufactured in the United States of America
06 05 04 03 02 01 00 99   5 4 3 2

Library of Congress Cataloging-in-Publication Data
Lemann, Nancy.
    Lives of the saints : a novel / Nancy Lemann.
        p.   cm. − (Voices of the South)
    ISBN 0-8071-2162-2 (pbk. : alk. paper)
    I. Title.   II. Series.
PS3562.E4659L5   1997
813' .54−dc21   96-50170
                                                         CIP

The paper in this book meets the guidelines for permanence and durability of the
Committee on Production Guidelines for Book Longevity of the Council on Library
Resources. ∞

*Then I climbed the sharp hill
that led to all the years ahead.*

EVELYN WAUGH

To
S.A.M.

LIVES OF THE SAINTS

All in all, Henry Laines' wedding was one of the worst events in my experience, tragic in society. Everyone that I have ever known was there, plus a party of out-of-towners whose broad Memphis and Charleston accents shocked me, although we were the same, Americans far from that hub of the universe along the East Coast.

Everyone had breakdowns at this wedding. Including the bride and groom. Especially the bride and groom. Crowded parties like at the Stewarts' often can be known to Bring On Breakdowns. Especially if the Stewarts are the hosts.

I went into this wedding armed with a philosophical acquiescence I had learned from the poets, but I found in society their principles did not hold weight. Everyone was too drunk. Everyone was unglued.

It used to mean so much that the poets were a friend to man in other woe than ours, afar from the sphere of our sorrow—but my quotations are confused. I don't know them anymore. Henry Laines would remember them. He knew all about it. Henry Laines was much admired by some, a kind of local hero. By profession, he was a starving artist, and by temperament, a bachelor. By that I mean that his icebox always held just one item at a time, something rancid, like an old head of broccoli residing in the freezer, so that he could try to save it.

I couldn't talk to him anymore. I could only listen. Then he would look at me as though I had just fallen out of a tree. All those people, all those catastrophes, not to mention breakdowns, at the wedding, made me lose the words of the poets. It was a Very Long Party.

The orchestra was playing old-time jazz, scratchy and remote, with people screaming in the background, and screams of laughter. The party of out-of-towners from Charleston was collected in a corner of the dance floor, which otherwise was not crowded, as most people were out in the garden and in other anterooms inside, in separate, tired, exhausted groups.

Brows were being mopped with white handkerchiefs, among white summer suits and seersucker suits, against a profusion of green in the Stewarts' garden. Everything was green and sumptuous and still, with green-and-white striped tents set up and the principals wearing white tie and tails. There were deck chairs set up in the garden, with people reeling around among them. It was stiflingly hot. Elderly gentlemen in advanced stages of disrepair were sitting in a row of deck chairs at the far side of the garden, all in their white summer suits.

The wedding was at three, and the reception started shortly after, but showed no signs of abating, though it was almost ten.

Henry Laines was screaming my name at the top of his lungs on the dance floor, not unlike the way he used to scream for Mary Grace, his bride, in the garden of his house at night. No one thought it was unusual that Henry Laines should be screaming my name instead of hers at his wedding reception on the dance floor, because everyone was too drunk to care. That is what it is like at parties where everyone is too drunk.

It was like slow motion when Henry Laines began to scream my name; a certain hush came over the dance floor, and a few people, particularly Claude Collier, gave Henry Laines a funny, somewhat pitying look from across the room. I noticed that. Claude Collier stood with his hands in his pockets, calmly contemplating the scene. His brow was furrowed, and he was squinting slightly. He was chewing a straw.

The rest of the dance floor was populated by the party of out-of-towners from Charleston, who threw some inquiring looks in Henry's direction and then lapsed back into their oblivion.

"I think Henry is falling apart," Claude Collier said to me.

Henry Laines had already had two breakdowns since the ceremony.

"It's been a long day. He's tired. He's falling apart," said Claude mildly in a calm tone, slightly deadpan. Then Claude Collier looked at me intently. Claude Collier made the world seem kind.

It was a night in the spring, though in New Orleans you can hardly tell the season as it's so often hot. A sweltering night in October can be just the same as a sweltering night in April, for in New Orleans the seasons have only subtle differences, unlike in the North. It was balmy old New Orleans weather in the tropic spring, and everything was green and overgrown.

Henry Laines was standing in the middle of the dance floor rooted to the spot. He was wearing white tie and tails, which were somehow ill-fitting and shabby, although he had a white carnation in the buttonhole. He looked unwell and was sweating, his face covered with sweat, in the unpleasant heat of the sweltering April night. He was then thirty-five years old. Henry Laines always had a slight touch of squalor. It always touched my heart.

We used to hear Henry Laines scream at his girl friends, different ones at different times, in the apartment across the garden at night from his house—"BECAUSE I LOVE YOU, GODDAMNIT!"—and then pots and pans would come clattering down the stairs, followed by "I LOVE YOU, GODDAMNIT!" I always used to think it was great, Henry Laines' wild declarations of love, with the pots and pans clattering down. Or, maybe, I didn't know whether to think it was great or horrible.

I used to live in the slave quarters behind Henry Laines' house, often cowering at the sounds that issued across the garden from his apartment. I never thought that he would marry. To me, he was the perfect bachelor. With crashes and music and women across the garden in his house, with the pots and pans clattering down.

Henry Laines looked older than his years. But, on the other hand, he always kept "that soaring quality which usually leaves a man at thirty." He was a foppish dresser, and would always emerge from the squalor in which he existed with some foppish eccentricity, or would be off to balls wearing white tie and tails.

-)≡(-

I surveyed the crowd, looking for people I knew. Mr. Walter Stewart, father of the bride, was an extremely large and loud man.

He could be heard above the crowd. His blond wife was a person of whom he appeared to be only remotely fond, or even aware. She could spend an entire afternoon talking about what hat she wore when she was fifteen. She could also tell you who married who in the entire city and what scandals they caused. But her frivolity was heroic. She did it on purpose. Her husband ignored her, and she had lost her favorite son in a car wreck. She was an intelligent woman, but she just talked about what hat she wore when she was fifteen. Only the truly gallant, so it is said, are light-hearted in adversity.

Mrs. Walter Stewart did her duty in the world, without inquiring why, as though spurred on by the largeness of her husband and three remaining sons. Mr. Stewart had just recovered from his third heart attack. He was so large and robust it appeared he might endure a whole succession of heart attacks. He also had five hysterical, vivacious daughters, their husbands, their screaming children, and their black maids, all of whom were strewn in a panorama throughout the house.

His aging mother had come to live with them after his first heart attack. She was a woman with a grand and remote past. But quite like her daughter-in-law—because there was no subject dearer to Mr. Stewart's mother's heart than the subject of what hat she wore when she was fifteen. They both spent many hours talking about details of girlhood attire, and other lame-brained elements of clothing through the decades.

·─>⊞<─·

Mr. Walter Stewart came up and put his arms around me. I couldn't reach his cheek to kiss, but tried awkwardly, and succeeded in pressing my glasses lens into his cheek.

But he took my hand and said, "You are very dear to me, young lady."

Large, beefy, and handsome, with watery blue eyes, he invited me back into the house—or rather, ordered me in. Then he took me into his duck-hunting room and showed me his rifles. I politely admired his rifles, and he launched into a soliloquy about hunting and the thrill of the chase. Then he went off to stand on the front lawn of his mansion, where he called out to passersby—"My daughter is a delicate magnolia blossom!" or "I love my baby doll!"—in his gravel-voiced baritone. "She's my favorite, you know!" he advised the public. "She was always my favorite."

→⋙⋘←

The best part of the night was when Claude Collier came up and turned my collar down and called me Darling.

I have found there is something about a turned-up collar that makes people want to turn it back down. It grips them with an overpowering desire to come over to you and—with a glazed, fond look in their eyes—turn your collar down.

But when Claude was turning my collar down, he held it so shockingly tenderly that I had to look away, as though you are so far from those you love that you drift out of time. I couldn't even look at him because it was like that. It was also shocking because it was uncharacteristic. I had known him for so many years.

"Everyone is falling apart," he said. He spoke in his calm dead-pan. "But you're so pretty that it's taking advantage of some of that which would have been wasted," he added incoherently.

In the time that it took me to drink one gin and tonic, he would drink three. Alcohol was no stranger to him.

"No no," I said, "Don't say a thing like that."

Then he called me Darling.

He was wearing a yellow tie, a wrinkled dark blue suit, and an overstarched white shirt. His tie was strewn over his shoulder and around the back as though it were strangling him. He was absent-minded, disheveled, not vain. Vanity is worse than any vice, in my opinion. He had none. It was this which made him handsome.

He took my hand in both of his, and looked at me with his benevolence—a look that wished you so profoundly well, it seemed to predict that life was a swift, sure-footed journey.

→⋙⋘←

"The thing I remember most vividly from my youth," Mrs. Stewart the elder was saying to me, "is that little red hat which I wore in the summer of . . . 1912. It went with a blue suit. I remember it vividly," she said, her eyes rapturous. We were talking about what hats we wore when we were fifteen. What shoe sizes her friends wore in 1910, minute details of clothing, recalled to her the Mystery of Life and filled her with the greatest zest. She was in her eighties and had a perfect memory for her attire through the years, but could not remember things in a normal conversation.

"What do you do, Louise?" she said to me.

"I'm working in a law firm now."

"Oh, how nice."

"Well, it isn't exactly the nicest thing you could ever think of, but it's—"

"Now, what was it again, dear—what was it that you do?"

"Oh. Well—that is, I work in a law firm."

"Now let me just get this straight. You work in a law firm . . . downtown?"

"Yes, uh, it is downtown, yes."

"Well, why don't the young people want to just stay home and read?"

"Oh, I wouldn't mind doing that at all."

"You wouldn't? Well, I think that's very nice. Do you work, though?"

"Do I work?"

⋅⋗▧⋖⋅

Claude walked up and started overwhelming Mrs. Stewart with his politeness. He was always polite. It was one of his greatest traits. It is hard to be truly polite. It is an elegant trait.

I felt like I was going into a stupor. I could hear Mr. Stewart quoting from a famous book he owned that he always quoted from, which was a history of the battles of the Civil War written entirely in verse. It filled me with dread.

"Let me tell you something about women," I could hear Mr. Stewart saying. "You have to treat women gently because they're weak. Young girls should be sheltered. They shouldn't be allowed to have affairs. One affair, and they're ruined. I pity women. After one affair, they're ruined. Who would want them?"

Oh, God, I thought. He was a law professor and had a tendency to lecture on all occasions. He often aired his private views for the benefit of large groups. He took a particular relish in quotation. I could hear him quoting from the Bible:

" 'Woman, thou shouldst ever go in sackcloth and mourning, thy eyes filled with tears. Thou hast brought about the ruin of mankind.' "

He was looking remorsefully into the eyes of some poor unsuspecting woman standing next to him, to gain a histrionic effect. As though off in a reverie, he turned dazed eyes on his youngest son.

"Peter, I'll tell you what Jeb Stuart used to say." Mr. Stewart looked raptly off into space. " 'All I ask of fate is that I may be killed leading a cavalry charge.' "

-->>❒<--

The rooms were hung with Mr. Stewart's pictures of horse races and hunting dogs and generals. There was a life-sized portrait of Napoleon. Mr. Stewart led the party in his vicinity to the duck-hunting room to look at his rifles.

I went back to Claude and Mrs. Stewart the elder, who were sitting there drinking like a couple of fish and chain-smoking. Every so often Mrs. Stewart lapsed into a coughing fit brought on by her dissipations.

Claude leaned over to me and said in a low tone, "I'm so drunk."

He had a little habit of calmly and obliviously shredding napkins, matchbooks, and cigarette packages, and he had filled about three ashtrays with shreddings. You could always tell a room in which Claude had recently visited, because its table tops would be strewn with shreddings and chewed pencils and chewed straws and other wreckage.

"Stop shredding things," I said.

He took a pencil out of his pocket and started eating the eraser. Then he leaned over to me and confided, "I'm so drunk."

"I seem to remember hearing this conversation somewhere before," I said.

He picked up a napkin.

"Mrs. Stewart? Louise? Can I get you a drink?" Claude said loudly.

"No, thank you," I said significantly.

"Why, I'd love a drink, Claude," said Mrs. Stewart gaily.

He walked over to the bar and got the drinks. He joked around with the bartender, apparently having a strong bond of affection with him. Then Claude went over to the bandstand and told some kind of joke to the orchestra, who all appeared to be in stitches from it, having found it so unbearably hilarious, whatever it was, that they stopped playing and were all drooping over their seats in hilarity.

A group of debauchees were sitting in a corner by the bar with napkins tied on their heads and loaves of French bread stuck in their breast pockets, even though they were grown, twenty-eight-year-old men. "CC!" they screamed when Claude drew near, and everyone seemed to get very maudlin, with Claude bending down to shake hands, as though he hadn't seen them in a Very Long Time, as opposed to one minute ago.

The men were calling each other *sweetheart* and *baby*. Things seemed to be getting more maudlin. Claude walked up and down the hall among the revelers strewn in chairs along the walls, stooping down to shake hands with elderly men. Then Claude did jokes for his cronies, which put the entire party in even more of a slapstick mood than even the napkin-heads had been in. Devil-may-care, that was their attitude, after Claude got through with them.

But I saw him take a pack of cigarettes out, and his hands were shaking so badly when he tried to light the match that I saw him give it up and leave off trying. He put the package surreptitiously back in his pocket.

❦

Mrs. Stewart, next to me, was talking about who married who in 1910. Claude returned and sat down, chewing a bottle cap. Pensively, he took out the pack of cigarettes and started to divide the foil part from the paper part, leaving a pile of strips on the table.

"Could you please tone it down a little?" I said.

"Yes, enough silliness," he said. "Now I must suffer." He clutched his throat and pretended to be having a strangulation fit.

"If that weren't so amusing, one might laugh," I said darkly—but confused.

"I find it so terribly amusing," he said, "that I'm terribly amused. I find this terribly amusing."

"I find this rather immature," I said. "If this weren't so unbearably immature, maybe I would—"

"I feel very mature right now. I feel extremely mature."

He put his hand on my knee. I just stared at it in a stupor.

"The way your slip was showing," he said, "it reminded me of the South."

Mrs. Stewart the elder was just sitting there with a rhapsodical expression in her eyes. Probably recalling the famous pink kid evening bag she used to carry in 1915. Suddenly, there was a booming voice above the crowd:

"LET US HAVE FAITH THAT RIGHT MAKES MIGHT, AND IN THAT FAITH, LET US, TO THE END, DARE TO DO OUR DUTY AS WE UNDERSTAND IT!"

It was Mr. Stewart.

His wife went across the room, I saw, over to his party.

"Walter, please," she said.

"Let the dead bury the dead!" Mr. Stewart boomed. "Poets, war—war, poetry—"

"Walter, please, come over here, dear," said his wife, who led him away from the group. She had an instinct for his breakdowns, such as the one that was swiftly impending. She took his arm. He stumbled. Everyone in the vicinity looked at the floor with embarrassed expressions.

Mrs. Stewart the elder was still staring off into space. She had that same glazed expression that her son had. Then she rose and was just standing there.

"Sit down, Mrs. Stewart, won't you?" I said.

She said ponderously and slowly, "I can't think of any reason not to sit down . . . If I don't sit down, I'll just be left standing . . . just be left standing here like I am now."

Their family was always having Breakdowns.

-->≒ЖЅ←-

"Sit down, Mrs. Stewart, won't you?" said Claude, standing up with his hand at her elbow. "Tell me that story about Monroe."

Mrs. Stewart perked up at the subject of beaux. She sat down again in her chair.

"Tell me about your beaux, Louise," Mrs. Stewart said zestfully. "I only had one man in my life," she said, "but believe me, I had many offers. Countless offers."

It was the story of the Countless Offers.

"Have I told you this story before?" she said.

"Why, no," said Claude, with his politeness. "Tell me about your beaux."

"Monroe always adored me," she said. "I don't know why. The Lord knows I did some stupid things. I lie awake these nights and think of it. I don't know how he put up with me. I know it must have annoyed him, some of the stupid things I did, but he adored me. I had a beau at the time who wanted to marry me, who never got over me. He came to call three times a week. He brought me orchid corsages. I was engaged to Monroe, and I remember the night I told him. I remember it vividly. Why, he was crestfallen. He never got over it. He . . . well, I have some secrets to tell, now that all my beaux are dead."

We sat in appropriately stunned silence.

"When I first met Monroe, you know, I was nineteen years old and he was thirty-seven. There was almost twenty years difference. But it didn't matter at all. Age doesn't matter. I met him on the train coming back from Point Clear, Alabama. I knew the first night I saw him that he was the one I wanted. I pretended, of course, that he couldn't have meant less to me."

"Are you going to Point Clear this year?" Claude said.

"Well, I may not be around for that," said Mrs. Stewart.

"Oh? Where are you going?" said Claude.

"I leave that to the Lord," she said, and lapsed into a majestic silence.

- ›≡‹ -

"Keep an eye on Tom," said Claude to me, getting up. Everyone was always telling you to keep an eye on Tom. As I've never seen a person who could get in so much trouble as Tom, I was a little concerned that it was now my job to keep an eye on him. Furthermore, he was the bride's old flame, or one of them. He was acting Extremely Peculiar. The last time I had seen Tom, he was lying down on the floor in a tormented crumple with a lamp shade over his head. He was wearing sunglasses and a suit made out of leather.

Then I found him sitting in his Lonely Splendor in one of the anterooms.

He trained a pair of smoldering eyes on me.

"Will you read the first chapter of my novel?" he said.

"Oh, really? That's great."

"It's dedicated to Mary Grace."

"Now, come on, Tom," I said, "get hold of yourself."

He stared at me smolderingly.

"Where *is* Mary Grace?" I said.

"She's probably in the bamboo grove having sex."

"The bamboo grove?"

"Well, you know, that's the type of person she is. She's the type of person who would just go out to the bamboo grove during the middle of a party or during her own wedding and have sex."

"She is? What? But—but—why the bamboo grove, though?"

"It's racy out there, Louise. It's sexy. Out in the bamboo grove."

"God," I said, stunned, wishing I were that type of person.

⇠⇝

Mary Grace Stewart, the bride, sailed past the parents of a boy whose life she ruined, who hated her for ruining their son's life, and she just sailed past, brave, undaunted, not caring. However, let me make it clear—not heartlessly uncaring, but on the contrary, specifically brave.

She was finally resolving her troubles, and the havoc she had wrought, by matrimony.

"They don't make them like Mary Grace anymore," said Claude's father fondly, passing by. He shook his head in amusement at the sight of Mary Grace, who left many souvenirs of herself in ruined lives between New Orleans and Boston, including, one might say, Claude. The whole wedding party was populated by the bride's old flames, not to say potential new ones. She had the spark of divine fire, which you find in a face not quite pretty enough.

Mary Grace Stewart was the type of girl you see being dragged screaming from a convertible sports car outside of the bar at the Lafayette Hotel at three in the morning by her father and brothers, and then, the next day, in the bank or shoe store looking as though she had been shedding a lot of tears. She wore conservative clothes with navy blue pumps, neat unwrinkled skirts, and alligator belts. I always used to see her standing in line at the bank looking like she was about to burst into tears, or going to buy shoes uptown with a vacant stare.

She always looked voluptuous and as though she were about to become hysterical. I could picture her bursting into tears at home while putting together some conservative outfit, her stockings hanging across a drawer and the room in disarray, an overgrown banana tree extending in through an open window, in this tropic setting, and the maid singing soul songs downstairs.

Maybe she was obsessed with clothes like her mother and grandmother were. Maybe it oppressed her, a kind of tragic triviality imposed onto her life. Maybe she was too bound by convention. Maybe she conformed to genteel Southern society's convictions without being particularly convinced that they were good.

You could never tell when Mary Grace might have a breakdown in the middle of society, and have to be led, weeping, from the room. Hysterics were no stranger to her. But people should be elated by the small things in life, by society at a wedding party in the garden, or just by sitting on the porch while looking at the rain slash into the azalea. If you are elated by the small things in life, I'd judge it means that you are truly happy.

- ❧ -

Mr. Collier, Claude's father, a mild and elegant man, was standing in a conversation at the bar. He was talking to a woman of about fifty, quite beautiful, but with a wildly crestfallen expression as though embossed onto her face, the lines of it were so deep. It was Mrs. Sully Legendre. She was married to a famous playboy.

Mrs. Sully Legendre had a jazzy way of talking, and would preface her remarks with *Kiddo, Baby,* or *Fella.* It seemed inappropriate, her saying to the dignified Mr. Collier, "Baby, just lemme tell you this..." and then she would make some jazzy, cynical remark. She would look at him inquiringly with her crestfallen face, but Mr. Collier was not forthcoming on the subject. He would never say anything bad about anyone.

Mrs. Legendre continued in a crestfallen vein, delivering some cynical maxims pertaining to marriage. Mr. Collier nodded stiffly, coughed, pretended to be thinking it over. He puffed on his cigar. He looked at her gently.

"Never marry a man with a weak chin, fella," she concluded grimly.

"Quite right," said Mr. Collier mildly.

--⟫▦⟪--

Mr. Collier was a man who always wore seersucker suits that he had had for about fifty years and which were always wrinkled and faded to a kind of yellow color. He and Claude looked alike in that their suits were always wrinkled and looked as though they had come from someone else's closet in a prep school in 1920. But that is about as far as the comparison goes, because Mr. Collier and Claude—they were not alike.

Mr. Collier was always trying to interest me in unexpected key changes in arias and oratorios. He was obsessed with Homer, and went around speaking in ancient Greek. He was conducting studies in Rhapsody. His ambition was to become a Rhapsode. What is a Rhapsode? What, indeed. It is a person who memorizes the entirety of Homer in the ancient Greek and goes around reciting it.

At the office, Mr. Collier would write papers for his eccentric club, which met monthly at Antoine's in the Quarter in a private room, where scholarly men in white tie and tails delivered to each other strange treatises. Mr. Collier was writing a paper called "Rhapsody." He would Xerox these papers and send them to me. Before that he wrote a paper called "Ecstasy." Imagine, the most mild-mannered man in the world writing something called "Ecstasy." But then when you read what he wrote, you found out that it was all about obscure metric configurations in ancient Greek. This, to him, was ecstasy.

Claude, on the other hand, never read a book in his life. But he was just as sweet-natured as his father was, both gentle to the bottom of their bones, without temper and without wrath. I never heard either of them raise his voice. They dreaded hard words; they dreaded scenes.

Mr. Collier was a tall man with posture excessively straight. He had a graceful frame, in his stature and, like his son Claude, in his bearing. He was increasingly thin. He had gray hair, in a sort of wild crew cut, with thick tufts of it sticking straight up rather oddly. His bearing was very stern. He was always dapper in his aging suits and bow ties, cutting quite a figure, an undeniably handsome man, if striking, if a little too stark, with his tufts of hair sticking up and his sternness.

President of the Louisiana Law Institute, formerly the judge at the Fifth Circuit Court, he was a man held in high regard. But I do not think he really liked the law. However, he did his duty in the world, without stopping to inquire if he liked it. Mr. Collier was the type of person everyone depends on, because he was steadfast. His old friends, types like Mr. Stewart, called him every day at the office to rave about all their crackpot Southern problems, and one word from Mr. Collier then restored them to at least some semblance of calm. His company was like a safe refuge and an uplifting climate.

❦

Mr. Collier and Mr. Stewart had been together from kindergarten through law school.

"How *are* you, Louis?" Mr. Stewart asked Mr. Collier in a confidential tone when Mrs. Legendre had left.

"Well, that's fine, just fine," said Mr. Collier vaguely.

"You look well," said Mr. Stewart.

"You can't tell a book by its cover, old man," said Mr. Collier, never one to accept a compliment under any circumstance.

Mr. Stewart directed a rather gloomy gaze on Claude, who was still sitting with Mr. Stewart's mother, apparently filling her with hilarity and inexpressible mirth. They looked like they were having the time of their lives.

Mr. Stewart looked at them darkly.

"I've been hearing some things about Claude," Mr. Stewart said to Mr. Collier. "I hear he's been spending a lot of his time at the racetrack."

"Claude is not using his abilities," said Mr. Collier.

Mr. Collier trained an eye of amused benevolence on his son Claude. Mr. Collier had a soft spot for Wastrel Youth. In fact, it was one of his favorite episodes in life. He always said—trying to get the lingo, in his dignified old age—that the young people should "find themselves."

"I'd like to see that boy at the law school, Louis."

"He's finding himself, Walter," said Mr. Collier, ecstatic. He loved wastrel youths, but he loved his sons to a degree approaching beatitude. The combination—his sons plus wastrel youth—was almost too much for him.

"He'll turn out all right," concluded Mr. Collier mildly, with an abstracted expression.

They said good night and shook hands firmly, with understated meaning, as is common among men who, despite their differences, have been together so long through the adversities of life.

···

I did not know what Claude was doing now or had been doing lately. He was thought to be in some sort of trouble. As is not so uncommon, in these or any times, he could not seem to find a profession.

People were worried about him. But Claude was not worried about himself, because he was the type of person who does not think of himself in the first place. He had no introspection.

He had an extremely sociable, high-hearted temperament, and claimed to be always having a great time. He did not have an intellectual turn of mind, no intellectual passions. However, he was what you would call a sterling character. He was the most sterling character I have ever known.

Whether you admire a man for his accomplishments or for his character is, I think, always a leading question. I myself tend to admire a man for his accomplishments. But I admired Claude. He had the indiscriminate kindness that is the meaning of generosity.

But he was also wild. He had more heart, if possible, than his father, and it was because he was wild. In this way, he got to know the world—better than I ever will.

※

The garden was still populated by the crowd, arranged in deck chairs around the green-and-white striped tents, in the steamy night. Some ancient couples sat in well-lit corners of the room beside the garden, which was now dazzlingly lit. Old-time jazz from the orchestra was wafting by, the instruments in languid unison, giving the effect of that buffoonish hedonism which you find only in New Orleans.

Claude was still sitting between Mrs. Stewart the elder and her daughter-in-law, who were discussing, at interminable length, the blue dress which one of them had almost worn.

Mary Grace was conducting a violent flirtation with George Sweeney in a corner of the garden.

As for the bridegroom, he was not in evidence. We found him sitting in an anteroom at an empty table crooning a song to some empty chairs. A stricken expression passed across Claude's face when he saw this. With a beleaguered step, Claude went over to Henry and talked to him for a while, consoling him. Then they both came striding out, and Henry, looking strangely sunny, paced resolutely to the French doors and then on outside to claim the bride.

"Love is like a garden," Claude commented to me. "It starts out all scrappy and puny, but then you nurture it, and then it blooms. It takes about fifty years, but finally it blooms," he said.

After delivering himself of this somewhat curious philosophy, he just stood there seeming tired and wise—though cheerful, which he always was.

"I'm falling apart," he said in his mild tender sarcasm.

"People fall apart easily here."

He then confided in me that his heart was constantly breaking into a million pieces on the floor when he saw something, for instance, like Henry sitting in the anteroom just then.

It was true that Claude was always constantly helping people who were having different types of breakdowns. As Mary Grace once put it, Claude Collier was the type of person who "would give an ant a funeral." It was very true. So if you can understand a person whose heart is constantly breaking into a million pieces on the floor, then you can understand Claude.

—⟫⬧⟪—

He was saying something about not being able to love just one person, but only being able to love about a hundred, because his heart was constantly breaking into a million pieces on the floor, and there was room in it for a hundred, but not for one. It didn't use to be this way, he said, but that was how it was now. I responded to this admission by claiming that I was exactly the same way—not having the slightest idea what he'd meant.

We went over to the bar. "Here come the boy I raised," said Chester, the old butler, in a reverential whisper.

"How are you, heart?" said Claude in that kind voice, and they shook hands.

In his suit and tie, Claude looked slightly unusual, so old-fashioned, a little stark, in his dark suit and overstarched white shirt, with a sodden, gin-like fragrance as though he had taken too long of a shower, a Southern habit originally brought on by fear of heat.

"That boy is an angel on earth," said Chester, watching Claude, practically with tears in his eyes.

Everyone's grip on his emotions was deteriorating.

"Stop, dawlin. Wait," said Chester to me. "That boy is the only chance you'll ever get to see an angel on earth."

—⟫⬧⟪—

Mr. Sully Legendre was weaving toward us. He had silver hair parted in the middle, making melodramatic wings on either side of his face, and a glamorous silver mustache. The society column in the newspaper referred to him as "the hyper-handsome Sully Legendre."

This hopeless burden fell on his wife. That girl got her heart broke.

He gazed at us with his heavy-lidded eyes, and then screamed in a maniacal voice, "BABY!"

Then he clasped me to his bosom.

"CLAUDE, DAWLIN!" he screamed to my companion.

Heads turned. Silence fell upon suddenly hushed conversations. It was as though Mr. Sully Legendre were returned, at last, from the Odyssey.

"BABY!" he screamed again in histrionic amazement and joy. "IT'S LOUISE BROWN!" he screamed, and stood riveted in amazement.

The man was plainly falling apart.

Claude made normal remarks and pretended that everything was normal—and Mr. Legendre subsided somewhat, though he still displayed the mock-amazed congeniality of New Orleanians confronted with the spectacle of one another.

⟶⟩⟨⟵

Mary Grace ran into the house in tears. Someone told us that Mr. Legendre had just crashed into the brick wall in the garden while attempting to drive his car. Claude said we should make him lie down. It was always like this in the Stewarts' house. Their household depended on emotional crisis to exist.

"Claude, dawlin, I heard you were moving to New Yawk," said Mr. Legendre while we led him upstairs. "Don't go, baby—New Yawk's not the kind of a place for you." Mr. Legendre gazed at Claude with his sentimental eyes.

"That must have been a rumor," said Claude. "I'm not going anywhere."

I hate rumors.

"Don't go, dawlin," said Mr. Legendre. "Come and have a drink with me next week and I'll tell you why you shouldn't go. Louise, dawlin, come and have a drink with me next week and I'll tell you why Claude shouldn't go. We can go to the park and just sit under a tree."

I would love to go and have a drink with Mr. Legendre and sit under a tree.

⟶⟩⟨⟵

We got him into one of the rooms upstairs and made him lie down. There was a packed suitcase by the bed which was filled with summer whites. Apparently mistaking it, in his stupor, for Claude's suitcase for his departure to New York, Mr. Legendre gazed at it from the bed.

"Starched white pants from Louisiana," he said sadly. "They won't understand that up there in New Yawk."

Then he passed out—not realizing, perhaps, the Profound Truth of his remark.

"Everyone is falling apart," said Claude.

—>⦿<—

I heard Mary Grace's voice:

"Jane, can I have some crème de menthe?"

There was a silence.

"No, Mary Grace, you cannot have some crème de menthe," said a sober voice, that of Mrs. Collier.

There were some muffled voices. There was a crash.

"I LOVE YOU, GODDAMNIT! BECAUSE I LOVE YOU, GODDAMNIT!" Henry's voice could be heard to scream from the vicinity.

—>⦿<—

Mr. Stewart was delivering another lecture on The Woman Question.

"Why, Walter," interrupted his wife, "how can you?"

"Barbara, Barbara, you'll never understand." He glared at her. "Men have ambitions, where women just have longings."

No one tried to argue, as they had all known him for decades. It was just his personality.

—>⦿<—

The reception was drawing vaguely to a close.

In the garden, there were gin and tonic and lemons and limes all lined up neatly in rows on a table, in readiness, and empty chairs— in the garden in the glittering night, under the monumental palms and oaks. Of that neighborhood, I could never tire. The antebellum houses—stony, impassive, still—and the monumental palms and oaks gave the place an unrelenting beauty.

They say April is the cruelest month—and maybe it is so. But it is not so in the tropics. It is not like the North, where spring comes like an idiot whose wake is strewn with garish flowers. The New Orleans spring is more subtle, and gentle to bear. Everything remains the same throughout the year, overgrown and green.

Then I saw Mary Grace in her traveling clothes, standing under the oaks in the garden, appearing to be having some sort of breakdown. Claude was standing there with her, with that stricken look on his face that he got when people were having breakdowns. I heard her say things only a drunk girl would say. Only a girl who was very drunk would say them. It was one of those swift and irrevocable moments during which someone's whole life is ruined. But Claude stood there stalwart and tall, with something understated in his eyes.

He took her face in his hand and said something, which I could not hear, but I do not doubt that he gave her kind advice, and that he wished her well.

--)ɛɕ--

Henry Laines was also falling apart. He was made that way. He was made to scream wild declarations of love to women in dressing rooms and gardens, and then throw pots and pans on them. And then he was made to get in rages and have jazz music and crashes coming out of his apartment across the garden and have nothing in his icebox except an old head of broccoli.

Life ran high in Mary Grace, and I admired her for that—it takes generosity to love, no matter what the circumstance, and she had loved many. But she was in a state of Total Chaos, among the madcap palms and honorable oaks, as society shed its bloodshot eyes upon the scene.

--)ɛɕ--

Everyone was leaving. The wastrel-youth contingent was making plans to meet later at the Lafayette Hotel for binges.

I was walking down the Garden District street, watching everyone "tank up," as my companion put it, in their cars, in alleys, and walking down the street, everyone with their plastic cups and glasses washing liquor down their throats. People were sitting in parked cars about to take off, but pouring liquor down their throats, first.

Tom, the bride's old flame, was strewn upon the ground, tangled up in the wires of his Walk-Man, passed out underneath his car.

So when the wastrel-youth contingent had departed, the old sat at tables in the house, with some of the men in tuxedos, against the ancient walls, with brandy glasses and cigars, a more than pretty sight, and looked back to view with fond dismay the crises of their own youth.

--➤✸✦--

The day after the wedding I slept until three-thirty in the afternoon. The telephone woke me up. It had to ring thirteen times before rousing me from my stupor. It was Claude Collier.

I did not know what Claude was doing now, or had been doing lately. I had just got back from college in the East, and had not seen much of him. But I had heard. The Lord alone knows where he had ended up the night before. Claude was always wild. However, as I have already said, he was what you would call a sterling character, and he was the most sterling character that I have ever known.

It is odd, the mixture of virtue and vice. No matter how many binges he went on, or what other things he did that I heard about, he had more ethics in his little finger than I could probably ever have. There are two kinds of people in the world, the kind who would never sit around talking about honor because they intrinsically have it, and then there is the type who would sit around talking about honor all the time, but who does not actually have it.

Though Claude would never use that word *ethics* in a million years because he was not the type of person to talk of things like ethics, he had more of those things in his little finger than I could ever have. He was wise in the heart.

But a lot of times lately I heard that he was acting pretty strange. I heard he was hanging around with wino lunatics and racetrack habitués and other weird types of wrecks.

-->⫸⚎⫷--

Claude was not solitary, or he could not tolerate solitude. Where he was, there was a party. But this is what I mean when I say he was generous. I wish that I could be more like him. But I am the opposite. We were like night and day, he and I.

At his apartment, there would always be a stream of visitors, ranging from his old friends in olive drab suits and seersucker suits and bow ties, to wino lunatics. Often they were in some kind of trouble, especially those in the former camp, for sometimes the well-heeled suffer more, and they leaned on Claude.

The telephone constantly rang. He always had dependents in his entourage, which is the sign of the generous.

I do not often see intrinsic kindness and responsibility like this in men. That is why I looked up to him.

Even if he spoke in platitudes, which he often did, he still would turn peoples' problems into a calm simplicity, a dear simplicity of his. He could take chaos—though not his own—and turn it into a calm simplicity.

It was that he listened so intently, that he understood. He was not lofty, or he did not tend to philosophize. It was not like that. It was the air about him, gentle and uncorrupt, some steady, noble thing. He was constant. He was steadfast. If you were his friend, you were his friend for life.

Then he was always cheerful, ridiculously, no matter what the circumstance.

-->⫸⚎⫷--

Some people were worried about Claude. But he was not worried about himself. The only thing he would ever say about himself was how normal he was. I remember very well a few months later sitting on the banks of the Charles River in Boston in tan deck chairs, with Claude looking calmly to the river of that Northern town, still saying he just couldn't believe that someone as normal as he was could have gotten into so much trouble and have spent all his time at the racetrack in New Orleans, where he hung around with wino lunatics, dissipated businessmen, crooked politicians, demented young lawyers, debutantes, alcoholics, and sleazy men with black-and-white checkered sports jackets and hacking coughs.

"Like all men with a future before them, he wallowed in inexpressible idleness" in his youth. But on the Charles River, he sat in his tan deck chair and looked calmly to Boston, with his optimistic blue eyes, in that brilliant, golden, cold air.

The Northern air was somehow more noble.

--》蹴‹--

Claude had never been to college, or rather he had no degree. He had gone for three months to the University of Virginia, but had been asked to leave after three months because of a scandal—blurred events that involved Claude accidentally lighting a girl's hair on fire at a party. Then, too, he never read a book in his life, least of all during three months at college.

His father got him a job as a page for a senator after that.

But after six months, Claude went up North to travel around and see things and wallow in Inexpressible Nothingness, until his father had to come and get him.

Claude returned to Washington in a van to collect his property, the entirety of which was then stolen one night in Memphis on the way home. His solution to this crisis was to go immediately to a debutante party in Texas, where he slipped on a banana peel at the party, which gave him the idea for a shrimp-peeling invention which was patented and which still brought income. But this seemed to have an adverse effect on Claude, because it was when he was making this invention that I first found him sitting in a room surrounded by bottles and acting detached and strange.

It seemed he could congratulate himself for nothing, and was only really in his element when he was making jokes and cutting up and cheering other people up, and holding them together, instead of himself.

He was not proud, for instance, of his invention. He had no self-love or pride. Though I admired his lack of vanity, it was this which held him back.

--》蹴‹--

There are some who say that defeat from the Civil War is still writhing in Southerners, filling them with self-loathing. I think there is actually some truth to this, though Yankees get mad when I say it.

⋅⟫⊠⟨⋅

Then to put it differently, he was a man who had, at some juncture, come to know himself, and therefore had come to despise himself, and therefore was deemed worthy of the name: wise.

⋅⟫⊠⟨⋅

The day after the wedding Claude came to my apartment. I was fixing breakfast—Carnation Instant Breakfast. He had on khaki pants several sizes too large and an overstarched blue-and-white striped shirt, the kind that looks like it came from one's father or brothers in the dim, more endearing past. But his gentle fading blue eyes had the look of someone who is not afraid—and with his posture straighter than an arrow, Claude had that slightly stern bearing he got from his father.

He politely watched me while I read the newspaper, which he'd brought. He did not speak. He had an air of observant logic, just watching me read.

"My eyes are killing me," I said. "I read like a fiend."

"Well, read like an angel," he said mildly, not taking his eyes off my face. "You're too interested in glamour," he said suddenly. "You socialize too much. You go out too much. You stay out too late. You drink too much. You should just be a simple, regular person. You should go to bed at eleven every night. You should just come home from work and cook, do the dishes, and just be a regular person. You shouldn't eat Carnation Instant Breakfast."

I received these stunning recommendations in silence. Then I said, "You're the one who needs that advice."

"No no, I'm just a regular, normal guy. Who leads a regular life."

"Oh, God."

"It's youth—it's just youth," he said looking at me, mild and unintelligible.

"What is?"

"Your behavior."

"What behavior?"

"You're so young!" he raved. "You're so innocent," he said. "How have you really been? I haven't really known, these past few years, when you were away at school. I heard you had a breakdown," he added in a kind voice, solicitous but cheerful, as though it interested him especially. "Breakdowns?" he said. "Tell me about your breakdowns. That's what we're all about down here," he said. "Breakdowns."

He had dazzling blue eyes, which looked at me with that benevolence, or seemed to look down through many years, as though he had the wisdom of the old.

Breakdowns. That was Claude's theme.

"No, no, I haven't had a breakdown," I said. "But what about you?" I said. "I thought I heard you had to go to the hospital. I heard you stopped drinking there, a year ago. I mean, speaking of breakdowns. And what's this about you moving to New York?" I said.

"How's that?"

"You know, when Mr. Legendre said. When he said he heard you were planning to move to New York."

"Planning to move to New York. Not quite, dear. My brother needs me here. I have to look after him. I have to look after you. I have to look after things here. Maybe some time," Claude said.

"What was going on between you and Mary Grace at the wedding?" I said.

"How's that?"

"Before they left, when she said those things, when she was drunk. You know."

But it was useless to think that he would tell me her secrets if they were not meant for me.

"What is it about Mary Grace?" I said. "I mean, what is she really, really like?"

"What is she really, really like?" Claude said. "Well, let me see now. What is she really, really like. That's a hard one." He shook his head. He gestured with his hand, as though trying to find the word. "Mary Grace—" He stopped again. "She was the wildest thing that existed," he concluded, and in the way he shook his head and gestured with his hand, I could tell that he had loved her once.

-->B<--

Claude reached into his pocket absently and handed me a pack of gum. It was a hot day. I got up and started scrambling eggs. He was standing a few feet away from me, tall and stark, looking at me through narrowed eyes, with a kind of stern, inscrutable affection.

"Are you by any chance scrambling eggs?"

"Yes. What of it?"

"You mean, you're just standing there scrambling eggs?"

"Yes. What is it, some kind of miracle?"

"What are you going to do next?" he asked as though it were intriguing.

"Take them out and put them on a plate. Do you want some?"

"Oh, no—but I mean, you, just scrambling eggs in the middle of the day, and here we are at your apartment, and everything is just normal, right?"

"Of course. It's normal. What do you mean?"

"I mean, you, just standing at the stove scrambling eggs, compared to what you will be doing two minutes from now, and what you feel like and what does it all mean."

He was shaking his head, bemused, at my scrambling-eggs capacity. Then he got up to go out on the gallery—except he tripped over a chair and tore his khaki pants from the ankle to the knee. Then his glass of gin and tonic slipped out of his hand and fell over the balcony and down to the bricks.

I just stood there at the stove, watching his catastrophes. These were Claude's normal catastrophes. Claude was accident-prone. He always had catastrophes. He also gave new meaning to the word absent-minded. Whenever he left on trips on airplanes, he would go off with other people's house keys and car keys in his pocket, causing huge Comedies of Error.

-->B<--

He was twenty-seven years old and currently was not working and was living off income from the invention, from betting at the racetrack, and from some investments he inherited, and everyone was always asking him what he was doing, to which he would answer, smiling brilliantly, "Oh, not too much," and start chewing a straw or tearing napkins into shreds.

--➤✠く--

I don't respect idleness in a man, of course. I don't just look up to someone who can get by without working. I respect a man who has accomplishments, and must therefore have worked hard to get them. A man should have a profession.

Claude was just Going Through A Phase. He just had not Found Himself yet.

St. Augustine had spent his youth in vice and dissipation, and look how he turned out.

But the idler's lot is a sad one, and this I do not deny.

--➤✠く--

There's a famous line in a story where there is a married couple and it is observed about them that she had none of the world's dark magic for him, but he couldn't live without her for six consecutive hours. My feeling for Claude was like the reverse: I could live without his presence—as I had just done, when I was away at college—for a whole duration of years between the ages of seventeen and twenty-two. But he had the world's dark magic.

I don't expect him to be near, I mean. He can probably live without me for six consecutive hours. It would not matter to me if I only saw him three times in five years—and it would still be with the understanding that if there are people like that in the world, then there is honor, for here was a fellow whom you could depend on to be kind as a steadfast, incorruptible rule.

--➤✠く--

I only went out to the racetrack with Claude once. We drove by the Quarter on Esplanade, everything green and curious in its tropical way, lush in the humidity, with steam rising up from the pavement in mists because of the heat. It did not seem like a normal American district; it never does, passing the Fifth African Baptist Church with the Gospel Soul Children practicing, the Crescent City Plantation Steak House with neon and white tile and green curtains in the private rooms, the Zulu Social Aid and Pleasure Club, Majestic Mortuary with neon lights and jazz, Seafood City where the employees come to work in tuxedos, and then the racetrack bar, Comeaux's, Grits Comeaux, Prop., who had a dead mummy hanging from the ceiling.

We only saw three races, and it was so boring and decadent that I fell asleep from psychological pressure. It rained on and off. Claude won eighty dollars on a three-dollar bet in the Exacta. He stood in the stands in his trench coat, chewing a pencil, squinting, making notes on the forms. But he looked like such an old-fashioned character, in his trench coat — tall and dark-haired — like a husband.

I tried to ask him about what he was doing. But he would not talk about himself. He was always reluctant to talk about himself. He did not have one ounce of vanity — the worst of the vices, worse than any of his, in my opinion.

--✶--

One time Henry Laines went out to bet on the horse races with Claude because Henry was always raving about how he couldn't pay his bills. In his inexplicable understanding of racing intrigue, Claude told Henry to bet on a certain horse in the Exacta in the last race of the day. Claude was looking at the forms, and he did not bet himself. Then he said that they should leave, even though the race had still to be run.

Henry protested, "I already placed my bet. The race hasn't started yet."

"Let's get out of here," said Claude like a criminal. "We can just get out of here and watch the sports on the six o'clock news. They give the outcomes. Then you can go back and collect the next day if you win. It's bad luck to watch the race you bet on. You should always bet and then leave without watching the race."

In line with this special wisdom, they went home to watch the news, and Henry's horse, in fact, did win seven hundred dollars on a bet that had cost fifteen dollars to place.

Henry was mute with amazement.

Claude watched the rest of the news, chewing a bottle cap, squinting at the screen.

Then it sank in, and Henry started grabbing everyone by the collar and telling them that he was going to be famous. That was the type of person Henry was. He was the type of person who, if you gave him half a chance, would start grabbing you by the collar and start screaming about fame.

Claude was just standing there still watching the screen.

-->⟩⟨⟨--

"Louise. Louise. Louise. Where were you last night?"

"I was at the Lafayette Hotel. Where were you?"

"What have you done to your hair? It looks different."

"It's called a bun, Claude."

"It's so pretty on you. A bun. I think I remember when you had one before. So you just had scrambled eggs. That was your breakfast?"

"Yes, for the nineteenth millionth time. Scrambled eggs. That's the nineteenth millionth time you've asked me about it."

"So you had scrambled eggs. You. Scrambled eggs." Claude Collier shook his head in wonderment, mystified.

"Yes," I said, "scrambled eggs, scrambled eggs, scrambled eggs, scrambled eggs."

"Could you, uh, reiterate that?"

His black hair was combed straight back from his forehead without a part. It was thin and lank. Some of it fell back over his ear rather wildly.

"Let me just drink you in, Louise," he said in his ridiculous deadpan.

"What?"

"I say, let me just drink you in."

"What do you mean? What do you mean, drink me in? I mean, I'm here all the time. You've been drinking me in for the past twenty years."

But he just sat there silently, presumably drinking me in.

"Would you like to go to a place near Des Allemands?" he said to me, looking at me kind of funny.

"What do you mean, a place near Des Allemands?"

"I know a place near Des Allemands, where we could go for a drink."

"Des Allemands? Well, let's not go out for any more stupid drinks at any more stupid bars," I said since I always had these remote glimmerings of rectitude.

"Louise, you're a kick," Claude said. I don't know why. "Come on, you want to go hear the Ink Spots? They're singing out on Airline Highway at the High-Lite Inn. It's on the way to Des Allemands. Want to?"

"The Ink Spots?"

"Yes, it's on the way."

"Oh, the Ink Spots? Aren't they kind of old?"

"Yes, they're kind of old. They're kind of old now, you're exactly right, but they still sing. They're singing out on Airline Highway. Want to go?"

"I love the Ink Spots," I said.

"Or maybe we should just sit around talking about the Ink Spots. That's what you'd probably rather do, knowing you," Claude said.

"Maybe we should just sit around talking about your career. Let's talk about your career."

"My career? I don't want to set the world on fire. I just want to start a flame in your heart," Claude said, quoting the Ink Spots.

~※~

And yet one felt such a melancholy or downright sorrow, as when there is something amiss, as when you wake up in the middle of the night or early in the morning suddenly, before it is time to wake up, with the distinct feeling that something is wrong—something with this life you are leading is very wrong—except you do not know what it is. It is a nameless wrong. This nameless wrong follows you wherever you go but you can't put your finger on it.

Under these conditions, there are times, late at night, or early in the morning, when you feel terror-struck.

When my heroes took an interest in me, I could not talk to them, and although they were kind to me, I could not accept their kindness. Claude Collier was a hero of mine. He had the levity of

the Southerner, a brave thing, being actually desperation masked
by levity. For some time, he was this way, nor did he change until
the Major Catastrophe.

❧

On the corner of Indulgence and Religion, in the Lower Garden
District, there is a violently pretty spot. It was Claude's parents'
house.

We walked across St. Charles Avenue as it turned dark, the
Avenue gentle and grand as it stretched down past view. You can
never see to its end until you come to the levee. You can only see
the arcade of green in the glittering night, under the elegant oaks,
and madcap palm trees raging at the side against a cobalt sky.

On the corner I mentioned there is Lafayette Cemetery, with its
aisles of whitewashed vaults. Directly across the street is Com-
mander's Palace, with its green-and-white striped awning and
Victorian turrets and balustrades, the palmetto garden lit up at
night, and dazzling white neon lights running all the way around
the roof. On the other two corners are antebellum mansions sunk
awry on their foundations, the pavement being crooked from the
weight of monumental oaks.

❧

Claude was in his late twenties. He had a little brother who was
twenty-three years younger. The boy was called Saint—his real
name was St. Louis Collier, the namesake of his father—because
he was so small and blond and wild. It was Mr. Collier who coined
the name. Saint was the type of child who is accident-prone, always
falling out of trees or breaking his head open on furniture. He
was often at the emergency room, where he would, obliviously,
drink Cokes the whole time, to satisfy his craving thirst for
carbonation.

Southerners need carbonation. Especially when they are growing up.

Saint Collier was so accident-prone that he was quite famous for
it, and when his friends came over they contracted this propensity
from him and fell out of trees or sprained their limbs. Frenzied

mothers often went to the emergency room from the Colliers' house with a small, bloody, hilarious child in the back seat of a car swilling Cokes.

-->►█◄--

Mrs. Collier spent much of her time mending socks or sewing name tapes for Saint, and calling out to him ponderously, as though up from a great abyss.

Mrs. Collier was always immaculately dressed in elegant clothes. Known for her vanity, she was imperious, malcontent, and fierce. She was a great pessimist and made many scathing remarks. Her philosophy of life was this: Why was she alone singled out to be so much worse off than everyone else?

But of course, in the actuality of the thing, Mrs. Collier was much better off than everyone else.

She was a Yankee girl Mr. Collier had brought down from Harvard many years ago, and she never got over the shock of New Orleans. As a newlywed, she wanted to wear baggy shirts and work with the professors in her department at Tulane, but somehow this was too unlike her generation, and also, there were always garden parties and witty intrigues and carnival balls. Mrs. Collier had to learn to cope with silver, with crystal, with entertaining, and with other things previously foreign to her. She was an upright Yankee girl who had gone to Radcliffe on scholarship and who then was brought into sudden and lifelong luxury by Mr. Collier of New Orleans.

A stern calm pervaded in their household—or I should say, a stern calm existed between Mr. and Mrs. Collier. The chilly, formal air between them, their manner with each other—they occupied a chilly corridor—I can't explain their dry behavior, their unearthly calm.

-->►█◄--

The central instinct in Mrs. Collier was a kind of harried motherly solicitude, though she always expected the worst, with a sardonic humor and a great air of gloom. She always tried to elicit from people their troubles and then, when they broke down and told them to her, she would exhibit a forced gaiety to conceal her inner horror, and her face would take on a blank look—as though she were trying very hard not to break down and take you to a mental hospital, where you could get proper treatment.

Mrs. Collier always thought everything was deteriorating and that everyone was about to crack up.

To everyone outside of her family, interestingly, she was a great hypocrite. No matter how awful she thought something was, she would say, "That's wonderful, dear!" Or if a friend of hers came over, she would say, "I absolutely adore that dress. Where *did* you get it? You're looking marvelous"—and then, when they had left, she would say. "Didn't she look just ghastly?"

—⟩⟨—

Mrs. Collier's attitude toward Claude was that he was in a Huge Crisis that could only be resolved by law school.

—⟩⟨—

"That new style in shoes is going to cause a lot of very serious orthopedic problems, Louise," said Mrs. Collier. "I can tell you that much."

We were sitting contemplatively in tan deck chairs set up in her living room. Mrs. Collier reached over to turn down my collar, and then settled back in her chair philosophically.

"You know, Louise, you and Claude are always yearning after vague things. You cherish illusions. I met someone the other day who was just like you—he yearned after vague things. You could tell, when you asked him about his job, that what he really liked to do was just to yearn after vague things. You're all living in a dream world."

"That's only the twelfth time you've told me that in the past two days," I said.

"Well, I'm just trying to make some headway," Mrs. Collier said. "I just want it to sink in. By the way, Mrs. Stewart has gone completely bonkers."

"How do you mean?"

"She's been drinking, she's exhausted." Mrs. Collier loved to think people were deteriorating, and loved to uncover their vices.

"Must this conversation degenerate into a gossip session?" I said. "Oh, Louise."

——>■<——

Crashes were heard in the distance, heralding the rapid arrival of a small, radiant, torturously sunburnt child who raced at breakneck speed into the room, knocking over a lamp.

"Oh, my God," said Mrs. Collier. "Goddamnit, Saint—come here this instant," she said.

He raced through the room and out of the French doors which led to the garden. Then he ran back in and stood before his mother, innocent and mute. He abruptly emitted a loud, blood-curdling shriek—and ran off again at the same breakneck speed, only to repeat this same process several times, which sent him into fits of hilarity.

"Don't aggravate me, Saint," Mrs. Collier said in a weary but menacing tone, her eyes closed. "Just don't aggravate me."

Trying to aggravate her, however, appeared to be the child's great mission.

"Saint, take that laundry hamper down," said Chester, the butler, coming in. "And fix me a cold drink," he ordered.

Chester had a calming effect on Saint Collier, and he shortly subsided—into a state of unearthly calm similar to his father's. Whether this calm side, or the wild one, was Saint Collier's most habitual or native state, I am not sure. I ask myself that same question about his brother.

——>■<——

"Mary Grace looked just ghastly at her wedding," said Mrs. Collier. "Didn't she look just ghastly? It would be impossible for anyone to look worse than she did," said Mrs. Collier. "Except maybe if you were her mother. If you were Mary Grace's mother, you would look worse." She paused. "I've got to get a grip on myself," Mrs. Collier said suddenly. "Why am I in this rat race? What is it all for? I am fifty-five. Soon I will be sixty. What is this rat race for?"

"What rat race?" I said.

"I'd like to be strapped to a bed for a year."

"Strapped to a bed for a year? What? God, Mrs. Collier, what do you mean by that?"

"I don't know. I just don't know," she said. "I'd like to be committed."

"Committed? Committed to what?"

"To the Jo Ellen Smith Mental Hospital."

"What? The Jo Ellen Smith Mental Hospital? Who's Jo Ellen Smith?" I said.

"She gives advice to mental patients on the radio," Mrs. Collier said. "She's completely bonkers."

"Then why do you want to go there?"

"You're right," Mrs. Collier said. "Why."

--)⚎⚎(--

A small black child making screeching racing-car noises propelled himself into the room. Byron, by name, was a friend of Saint's. He was about five years old. Byron was the type of person who would run into the house on weekday mornings and slide under the dining room table and make racing-car noises while everyone was trying to eat breakfast.

One of Byron's greatest pleasures in life was tormenting Mrs. Collier. He was quite small and got immense enjoyment from spending a lot of his time under the dining room table at breakfast or in the space between people's legs. Mrs. Collier would comment on his presence with a mixture of false gaiety and weariness.

As Mrs. Collier felt sorry for Byron, she always kept up an elaborate pretense of joyous vivacity when he was at her house.

Byron had gotten a toy racing car that you could drive around in if you were about three feet tall, and he would always "drive" over.

A small figure raced by, making screeching, gear-shifting noises.

"Byron just drove over, I think," said Mrs. Collier brightly.

When other people were around, she started her hypocrite mode.

"I got my car parked right out front," said a voice from under the coffee table.

"What do you mean, he *drove* over?" I said once, before I knew about it.

"Oh, Byron has a car," said Mrs. Collier in a tone to signify that she and he shared private knowledge. "Byron drives all the time," she said encouragingly.

She always tried to humor him.

"How is your father, Byron?" Mrs. Collier asked.

Byron was still under the table, but remarked, "He over in St. James."

"My Lord, dear, why?" said Mrs. Collier.

"He admitted to St. James for a case of nerves. My mama done boot him out the house so he could get an attack of nervous condition like he says, so they could cure him. He tried to strangle my mama."

"Byron, don't exaggerate," said Mrs. Collier, carrying on her conversation as though with no one, being as her listener retained his special place of honor underneath the coffee table.

Byron raced toward us and dived into the space, which was quite slim, between me and Mrs. Collier on the couch. I enlisted him in a game of cards, with which he soon grew bored. He sang in a soft Southern voice—

> *Mama in the kitchen, she cooking rice,*
> *Daddy on the front porch, shooting dice*

Saint sat nearby regarding him, rapt.

—⟫⟪—

Mr. Collier was standing in his garden wearing ill-fitting seersucker shorts, which came down well below the knees and seemed like relics from the war, navy blue socks with white bucks, and an old-fashioned sleeveless ribbed undershirt. This was his gardening outfit. Opera issued from a small tape recorder clipped to his belt. He stood lost in thought, in his garden. He looked thoroughly ridiculous.

"Good evening, sir," I said.

Mr. Collier liked it when young people called him sir. Every night before dinner everyone had to go up to Mr. Collier and say, "Good evening, sir," and shake hands with him, even small children.

"Louise," Mr. Collier said, and looked at me gently. "Fine, fine," he said.

"What are you doing, sir?" I asked as he stood there, lost in thought.

He made a remark in ancient Greek, with a high-minded, philosophical expression. "I know in my heart that one day Troy will fall," he translated, and looked into the distance with a faraway, resigned expression.

"Are you doing some gardening, sir?" I said.

"I'm trying to bring order out of chaos," he said mildly.

Sunday was his day of ecstasy—with gardening, opera, and ancient Greek.

"Well, I have to go cut some bamboo shoots now," he said.

"Why, sir?" I said.

"My bamboo grove. Bamboo. Quite important, you know. Bamboo is quite important."

Bamboo was also a source of ecstasy, perhaps. Mr. Collier always had eccentric, meaningless interests to which he was blindly devoted. But when you asked him why—why bamboo? why is bamboo important? why do you do that, sir?—he could never really say. This, I have concluded, is the sign of a true eccentric, for when you ask a true eccentric why he takes an interest in the things he does, he will not be able to tell you. When you ask him Why, the true eccentric does not know. He does not know why he does it. He just does it.

I left him in the bamboo grove and returned to the house.

⁕⁕⁕

Mr. Collier shortly followed me inside, a walking operatic aria, with music issuing from the small tape recorder clipped to his belt.

He went to his desk, which was piled high with bamboo collections, and regarded it thoughtfully. He began to separate the different sizes of bamboo shoots into different piles.

As I said, Mr. Collier was in his bamboo phase. Finally, Mrs. Collier said, with smoldering exasperation, "Louis, why are you doing that?"

To this he replied promptly.

"If I don't, who will?"

"Oh, God, Louis," she said.

"I'm trying to bring order out of chaos," he continued.

Saint straggled over to his father and stuck out his hand.

"Good evening, sir," Saint said.

"Ah, here is my little Saint," said Mr. Collier. Then Mr. Collier smiled, a thing which was somewhat rare. He just stood smiling at his little boy.

"What is this apparition? It's my little Saint," said Mr. Collier.

"Pop, what do you do all day?" said Saint, looking at the bamboo piles.

"What do I do all day? Well, I get my shoes shined. Then I go to the barber. Mainly, I listen to music."

"But Mrs. Poe said you work in a law office."

"Mrs. Poe?" Mr. Collier looked around in wonderment. "You believe everything you hear from Mrs. Poe? She is pulling your leg, my boy. Mrs. Poe is a notorious leg-puller. Don't you know when someone is pulling your leg?"

A kind of remote, glazed mirth passed over Saint's face. In fact, a mirthful intelligence beyond his years was there.

Then he slumped into a chair.

"There's a certain meteorite in the sky, and it's all made up of plasma," Saint said, with concern.

With that, Saint subsided into another state of Unearthly Calm similar to his father's, in which he remained for some time.

--》≈≪--

Claude emerged from the upper regions of the house and slowly entered the room, causing a silence. He was wearing baggy Bermuda shorts several sizes too large for him, an obsolete beach shirt, and a ludicrous apparatus called Acqua-Pac, for hangovers, attached to his head. Mrs. Collier regarded him in horror.

Taking off his headgear, which consisted of an aquamarine quilted mask in the shape of old-fashioned pointy sunglasses made of some shiny velour, which ordinarily he kept in the icebox, Claude smiled brilliantly at everyone and then walked over to his father.

"Good evening, sir," said Claude in his ridiculous, cheerful deadpan.

Father and son shook hands.

"You're up early, Son," said Mr. Collier. "It's only five. I thought you were in the arms of Morpheus."

Mr. Collier always became slightly madcap around Claude.

"He needs some coke spoons," said Mr. Collier. "Say, kid, got any Panama Gold? Acapulco Red? You need some coke spoons, kid," said Mr. Collier, not really knowing what any of these things were.

Mr. Collier was a notorious leg-puller. He always tried to kid Claude's friends about their Wastrel Youth. He solemnly produced from his desk a box of drug paraphernalia, elaborate contraptions of which he had only the barest understanding, given him by admiring youths who were the friends of his children and who were accustomed to Mr. Collier's Wastrel-Youth/Drug-Theme jokes.

Mrs. Collier stared at this exchange in horror.

→⊰⊱←

"Claude, your hair is sopping wet," said Mrs. Collier. "It makes you look like a Chinese opium smoker."

"Maybe that's what I am," Claude said. "Maybe I'm a Chinese opium smoker."

She just looked at him.

Claude wandered over to Saint and looked at his little brother with an odd, almost pedantic air.

"Are there any banana brains in this room?" said Claude. "Because I want to do an experiment on a banana brain. I personally believe I am standing next to a banana brain, and I do not mean you, Louise, my little cauliflower."

Saint dived into the vicinity of Claude's stomach, and then latched onto one of his legs.

"I can't walk, baby lamb," said Claude. "I can't walk when you do that."

Saint remained strictly attached to his brother's leg.

"Would you go to the drugstore for me?" said Claude to his leg attachment. "I want a banana brain to go to the drugstore and get some Alka-Seltzer for me."

"I'll go, I'll go to the drugstore," said a shrill voice from points leg-ward, who then raced like a shot out of the room, knocking a priceless ashtray off the coffee table.

"Oh, my God," said Mrs. Collier.

⋅→⋗⊠⋖←⋅

"I'm falling apart," Claude announced calmly, deadpan, standing melodramatically in the middle of the room.

I laughed.

"She's falling apart," he said, pointing at me.

Mrs. Collier regarded him intently, despairingly.

"This family is in crisis," Mrs. Collier said in her family's curious deadpan.

"Now, now, Jane," said Mr. Collier, "let's all keep calm," he said.

"I'm calm," said Mrs. Collier.

"Let's all keep very, very calm," said Mr. Collier.

"We're calm," said Claude.

"This family is made up of emotional cripples," said Mrs. Collier.

"It's good to be an emotional cripple," said Mr. Collier cheerfully. "I like being an emotional cripple. It's the only way to be. An emotional cripple." He puffed on his cigar.

"I'm worried about you!" said Mrs. Collier to Claude.

"Why?" Claude said loudly, but feigning nonchalance, as he tripped over Byron and knocked over a lamp.

"This is why!" Mrs. Collier said, holding up a pair of smashed glasses in one hand and some shards of priceless china in the other.

Then a bolt of lightning carrying a small package of Alka-Seltzer shot into the room.

"Thank you, babe," said Claude to Saint. "Everyone who wants to go to the French Quarter for breakfast tomorrow, raise their hand," said Claude, sitting down on the couch.

A small black arm came up timidly from under the coffee table.

"Darling, you'd better tell Byron good-bye now," said Mrs. Collier. "He'd better get home. It's time for dinner."

The two small banana brains stood together. "See you tomorrow, same time," said Saint to Byron. "Don't forget the code."

"Claude," Mrs. Collier slowly proposed, "what would you have done if I hadn't got your suit from the cleaners to wear to the wedding yesterday?"

"I would have committed suicide," Claude said. "My life would have been a pile of rubble."

"I would have committed suicide," said Saint shrilly, ecstatic.

Saint often imitated his brother.

"I would have thrown myself into the Mississippi River," Claude said. "I would have entered a mental hospital."

"I'm the one who is going to a mental hospital," said Mrs. Collier.

"Dinner is served," said Chester, coming in.

The Colliers were the last family in America to eat formal dinners served by a butler wearing a tuxedo. Even if no one was there except Mr. Collier, Mr. Collier would still eat like that, being served by Chester, while Mr. Collier sat alone, with the rain slashing into the azalea in the garden.

-->≫⬧⬧<--

"I'll be there in three-and-a-half minutes, if that's appropriate, Jane," said Mr. Collier. He looked at his watch. "You gals can start without me."

"I'll take the girls in to dinner," said Claude.

"Fine, fine. You take the girls in to dinner. The girls are probably getting hungry," said Mr. Collier.

"I'll take My Darling Girls into dinner," said Claude.

"Would you two please cut it out?" said Mrs. Collier.

-->≫⬧⬧<--

Saint started talking about bridges. He was Very Interested in bridges lately. Bridges were what made his Life Worth Living. He was studying bridges. Sometimes Claude had to take Saint out for a whole day to look at different bridges in the city. The theme was definitely Bridges.

"Do you, by any chance, know if there are any meteorites in the sky?" said Claude to Saint.

"Yes, and they're all made up of plasma!" Saint screamed.

"Hmm. Fascinating. Are you, by any chance, interested in bridges?" said Claude.

This of course reduced Saint to a pile of mirth-filled rubble. We had to assist him in to dinner.

-->≈<--

"Darling, could you please eat with a fork?" said Mrs. Collier. "That object on your left is known as a fork."

Saint reacted to this by slowly sliding his head down from the table until it could no longer be seen. He lay down in his chair horizontally.

"Darling, this is known as a dinner table," Mrs. Collier said. "That object in which you lie prone is known as a chair. Do you think you could bring yourself to sit in it like a normal person?"

Saint rolled his eyes into his head and pretended to be having an attack of strangulation.

"Jane," said Mr. Collier to his wife, "did someone escape from the insane asylum? Do we have an insane person in our house today? I sense that one of our party is going insane."

"Not insane—it's spastic," said Saint.

"Let's send him back to the asylum," said Mr. Collier.

"Saint, please take your legs off the arm of the chair this instant and sit properly," said Mrs. Collier.

"You are not riding a horse, Son," said Mr. Collier.

Every reprimand caused Saint a fresh episode of hilarity. He was dissolved into a writhing mass of total hilarity.

-->≈<--

"Tell us what you're studying in school, Son," said Mr. Collier.

"We're studying bridges," said Saint.

"What else, other than bridges, Son. We've had our fill of bridges."

"The Presidents," Saint said.

"The Presidents. What have you learned about the Presidents?"

"Well, they all had diseases," Saint said avidly, warming to his subject. "Did you know that Andrew Jackson had a weird disease where he drooled all the time? He had something wrong with his gums that made him drool all the time—kind of like throwing up, except with spit."

"Really?" said Claude. This was Claude's kind of subject.

"And Abe Lincoln had something wrong with his intestines all the time, and whenever he—"

"Darling," said Mrs. Collier, "I think you can spare us this unique information. Is this what they teach you in school?"

"Yeah," Saint said, starry-eyed.

Mr. Collier recited a cautionary passage in ancient Greek.

"Do you ever have thoughts like right now I'm sitting here and two hours from now I could be in the bathroom brushing my teeth and what does it all mean?" said Saint.

This curious inquiry was received in silence.

"That's an interesting thought, Darling," said Mrs. Collier, with a worried expression, after a pause.

"I wonder about that all the time," said Claude. "I was asking myself that just this morning. What does it all mean? Or what if your eyeballs fell out just accidentally like with the fish," he continued.

"Cut it out, you two," said Mrs. Collier. "Must you always have these idiotic conversations?"

"The inside of my face hurts," Saint announced. "Like behind my eyeballs. Behind my eyebrows."

"Maybe your eyeballs are falling out," said Claude.

"I don't find this funny," said Mrs. Collier. "Quite frankly this is uncalled for. I mean, some people don't think it's funny."

"I think it's funny," said Saint in a shrill, sing-song tone.

"Simmer down, Darling."

Then Claude suddenly started paying everyone elaborate compliments. He even complimented the lettuce, the furniture, the wallpaper, and the bricks and mortar.

"This lettuce is great!" Claude screamed. "This lettuce is so crisp. Louise, that dress, what does it all mean?"

"Let's all keep calm," said Mr. Collier.

"I'm calm," said Claude, "I'm perfectly, perfectly calm. I feel very calm right now."

"I'm paralyzed," said Saint sitting suddenly bolt upright in his chair. "My arms are paralyzed."

"Oh, my God—me, too," said Claude. "My arms are paralyzed, too. Take us to the hospital, our arms are paralyzed."

This produced uncontrollable mirth in Saint, who had to lie down again in his chair and gasp for air.

—>※<—

After dinner Mr. Collier went to the sideboard and started lighting several cigars. He lit one and set it down in an ashtray, then lit another, until he had six of them lit. Then he lodged the cigars between the fingers of his right hand, the remaining three lodged in his left. Thus armed, he proceeded to the library.

He stood stiffly at his desk, puffing on his cigars, testing one, then another, as the ashes fluttered down to the rug.

"Why are you smoking six cigars at once, sir?" Claude asked.

"Because it's Sunday, of course," said Mr. Collier.

He stood at his desk, smoking cigars and studying Greek verses, muttering to himself. There was a great deal of muttering, in ancient tongues, coming from his quarter. His wife remarked it ruefully. Mr. Collier's interests alarmed her, vaguely.

A bout of calmness descended upon Saint, who sat quietly listening to his father mutter in ancient Greek. Saint studied his father contemplatively, with a squinting, observant look and a curiously adult-like demeanor on the whole, as though he meant to figure the fellow out, once and for all.

After a while, Mr. Collier patted Saint on the head and said, with a gentle, abstracted expression, "My little Saint." He turned his head to one side, and looked at his little boy with a sweet, uncanny smile. "Good night, my treasure," Mr. Collier added then, with a sort of solemn gaiety.

—>※<—

"Jane," said Mr. Collier when they were alone, "you actually look happy."

"Is that so rare, Louis?"

He looked at her intently.

"It's more rare than Halley's comet," he said in the tone of a man much struck by something—or a slightly pleading tone, with profound sincerity.

However, Mr. Collier adored Mrs. Collier with the single-hearted adoration of the innocent.

---❯❯❮❮---

Mr. Collier had designed a plan for Claude to look after Saint, for the reason that, according to his judgment, as he was sixty-two years old and Saint was five, an unsound gap between paternity and its demands, he always thought he was too old to raise him. He looked into the future, and was thus a man of planning.

We were sitting by the garden. Mr. Collier was listening to the music and looking out into the garden.

"This is the saddest piece of music ever composed," Mr. Collier announced. He looked into the garden. "Can you identify this piece, Louise?" he said to me.

"The C Minor Mass of Mozart," I said.

He looked back at me, ecstatic. That was what really made him happy, if you could identify a certain excerpt, or speak in ancient Greek.

Mr. Collier sat in contemplation.

"What are you thinking of?" said Claude.

"I am thinking of your future," Mr. Collier said, "and what life holds for you."

Claude fell silent.

"Don't worry. Everything will fall into place by itself. Hard work, generosity, and put others above yourself—that is what you should do. Then everything will fall into your lap. I know it will."

What thou lovest well is thy true heritage?

---❯❯❮❮---

But I guess our true heritage was the Wakamba Club, because that is where we went.

The Wakamba Club was across the street from Claude's apartment. Pounding rhythms of Puerto Rican rhumba waltz music greeted one inside the Wakamba Club. In fact, the same rhumba waltz, over and over and over, as the jukebox was defective. Claude frequently socialized at the Wakamba Club. His neighbors, the macabre Brierre sisters, unusual relics from a dim debutante past, also did. Everyone knew Claude in the Wakamba Club, everyone loved him. He was a particular favorite. There was nothing Claude loved more than to socialize with wrecked types of weirdos like in the Wakamba Club. He would always be wildly gregarious, with a joke for everyone. His rooms were littered with relics from nights at the Wakamba Club. His matchbooks bore the legend: WAKAMBA, *Your Host: Mr. Emile.* This was how Claude enjoyed spending his time. There was this seamy underside to Claude's life, with the Wakamba Club and the racetrack and his motley admirers and dependents. He, who was born to such gentility, existed on its fringes, and was able to get on with all types of people.

--·)ᗐᗕ(·--

I had to go to work early the next day. I worked boringly at a law office, typing and going out to get Cokes for the clerks. They were all addicted to carbonation.

Southerners need carbonation.

The office was on the top floor of the Louisiana Bank Building on Gravier Street. One saw the strangest sights there, including people like Earl Battaglio.

My favorite person at the office was Mr. LaSalle, the office-supplies man and the man in charge of the mail.

Emile LaSalle. He would always rave about how he was going to quit. "I'm going to walk out. Right on the spot. I'm quitting next week." He would have a few beers at lunch and, when he came back, he would try to kiss me on the cheek and shake hands with all the lawyers as though he hadn't seen them in a very long time. He would come up to me and look me right in the eye, in great earnest, and say solemnly, "Bow wow." Then he would dissolve into hilarity.

He was full of stories about the famous. He told me he once sat in an opera box next to Mussolini during the war and that Mussolini had tried to marry his sister. Then he told me that Nathaniel Hawthorne once walked into a restaurant when Mr. LaSalle was a very small child, and Nathaniel Hawthorne went straight up to his sister and patted her on the head and said she was cute.

"You've got quite a sister, haven't you?" I said.

"Aw, yeah, I been hobnobbing in my time."

-->⚙<--

Then Earl Battaglio, the born-again Christian of the office, started talking about Hell fire. One of the partners had to call Earl Battaglio into his office and talk to him privately to get him to stop preaching in the office. Earl was twenty-five and had just gotten out of law school. Lately, his biggest thing was the fires of Hell and the torture of writhing in Hell and of being tormented by different kinds of torture throughout eternity.

He talked about it all the time. He would come into your office and start talking about it while you were trying to work. Or if you were trying to discuss Mr. LaSalle's sister, Earl Battaglio would come in and interrupt and start talking about the fires of Hell.

"I was speaking with the Lord last night," Earl Battaglio said to us in the mail room, "and he said to me, 'Earl, what would you do if your dog had rabies because it wasn't blessed?'"

"Beg pardon, Earl?"

"I say, I was speaking with the Lord last night, and He said, 'Earl, what would you do if—'"

"No, I got that part, Earl, but what do you mean?"

"What would you do, for instance, Louise, if your dog had rabies because it wasn't blessed?"

"What would I do if my dog had rabies because it wasn't blessed?" I said. "Well, I think I would take that dog, and I would burn it in Hell. I would take that dog and burn it in Hell with different kinds of torture forever in flames," I said.

"You know, you're not supposed to preach in the office, Earl," said Mr. LaSalle.

But Earl Battaglio said, "I was doing the dishes last night, Louise, and suddenly I realized that I had lost my credit card. So I said, 'Dear Lord, I've lost my credit card, and Lord, you know I need that credit card or else someone else's charges will go on it—so, Lord, will you help me find that credit card?' And as I was standing at the sink the Lord said to me, 'Earl, go look on top of the icebox—you left that credit card there yesterday.' Well, I looked on top of the icebox, Louise, and there my credit card was. So you see, the Lord is looking out for us."

Then he said he would bring me a book tomorrow by Mod Modeliste, the Cajun motivator, for special people trying to rule their lives.

"She has to get back to work," said Mr. LaSalle.

--➤≋⋖--

I was working on a special project at the office, which was proofreading an eight-hundred-page book called *Texas Business Law* written by one of the lawyers. They thought I would like it because they thought it was literary and I had just got back from college where I studied English literature, and they thought that since it was a book, it would be literary. But actually *Texas Business Law* threw me into splenetic fits of dull dejection. It took two months out of my life to proofread it and a lot of times I had to bring it home at night or even do it on weekends. The author's favorite phrase was when there was a case of negligence because someone was "off on a frolic of his own." Every other sentence was that phrase. Someone was always "off on a frolic of his own" except for me, who was always proofreading *Texas Business Law*.

I wished instead that I could be off on frolics of my own.

--➤≋⋖--

After work on Monday, I went by Claude's apartment. His room was populated by an ancient, toothless, and dilapidated black man who sat on the bed clutching a loaf of French bread; a dissolute and unemployable young man of twenty (namely Tom) who was wearing a Hawaiian shirt and old-fashioned pointy black sunglasses; and a five-year-old child who was attached to Claude's leg, namely Saint.

"Thank God, you're all right," said Claude to me when I walked in. "I was worried sick."

"You were? Why?"

"Well, I haven't seen you since last night—and, for all I know, something could have happened to you. Are you all right? Where have you been?"

"At work. Of course, I'm all right. What do you mean? Why?"

"Because I've been a wreck, worrying. I've been racked with worry. You have to call and let me know that you're all right."

"You're such a nut," I said. "If anyone should be worried, it should be me about you."

"Why?" Claude said, stepping forward, tripping over the child who was attached to his leg, who fell on his glasses and crushed them, while a part of the plaster of the ceiling suddenly began to come down in a huge dangerous crash, with plaster everywhere.

"Because weird disasters always happen to you," I said.

"Me? Disasters? Everything's fine here," Claude said, looking uneasily at the ceiling. "What is this? I have to call Miss Brierre."

Miss Brierre, an unusual relic from a dim debutante past, was the landlady.

"I already talked to Miss Brierre," I said. "Miss Brierre asked me to ask you if you could go out and fix the fuse box."

"Fine," Claude said. "Everything is just fine. Now I'll fix the fuse box," he said, detaching himself from his leg attachment and walking calmly, as though in some Zen state, across the room. "One thing at a time," Claude said. "Fuse box, then ceiling. Everything is falling apart. But don't worry. I've got this situation completely under control. Everyone stay here. I'll be right back. Don't move. Do you want a glass of water? Okay, I'll be right back."

I was just looking at him like he was crazy.

"I'se going along with you, Mr. Claude," said the ancient, dilapidated black man, after a thoughtful pause.

He went out through the back to the garden and politely started working on the fuse box. Miss Brierre was in the back apartment, hosing down her garden.

Claude waved.

"Did the light go on?" he yelled.

I leaned my head out of the window and watched them as the afternoon was waning in the garden. The garden was an overgrowth, a profusion of green. The iron lace was painted a fading, bleached pale green. Claude was absorbed in the fuse box and Miss Brierre kept trying to strike up conversations with him. She knew how kind he was, because she would always be there when he came politely through the garden and up the stairs to his apartment, and he would stop to talk to her.

Miss Brierre had a soft spot for Claude, as many who knew him did, because of the kindness in his face—disinterested, mild, and solicitous—pure kindness in the abstract, quite unmingled with anything else. He was "one of those gentle ones that would use the devil himself with courtesy." He was an uplifting person, no matter what he did, because he was simply better than most people in his heart, and you could look up to him. It set your mind at rest, to see someone like that.

--)≣÷-

Byron ran into the garden.

"What are you doing here?" I yelled down to him from the window.

"My daddy tried to strangle my mama," Byron said. "He tried to strangle her."

"Now come on, Byron," I said, "Don't exaggerate. What's really wrong?"

"I don't know," he said.

"You better go on home. They'll worry about you."

"But I can't cross the Avenue by myself because it has two lanes."

"I'll watch you across the Avenue. I'll come down."

"But I want to go to the store," he said.

"You should be going on home."

"But when I go home, I don't have anything to do." He started using that sing-song tone of voice that signifies in small children intense boredom and dissatisfaction with things. It means they are about to lie down on the ground and start writhing in torment and ask five-year-old existential questions, like Saint always did.

Byron said, "When I go home I sit in the chair, and then I play with the curtains. I just play with the curtains."

"Well, why don't you play in your car," I said. "Didn't you drive your car over?"

"No," Byron said.

"Why didn't you drive your car over here?"

"Because my sister ruined it," he said in a final pitch of anguish, and, true to my prediction, lay down on the pavement in a crumpled ball, writhing.

I went downstairs to take him in hand and watch him across the Avenue. I went over to the fuse box and told Claude.

"He was just standing down there so he could look up your dress," Claude commented.

••◦••

I was walking down Second Street with Byron. On the lawn in front of the Stewarts' house were Mary Grace's five hysterical, vivacious sisters, their children, their husbands all saying *Sugar, reach me my drink* and *Sugar, hand me that glass* — everyone screaming for the black maids, with vivid colors of black maids in white uniforms on the velvet green lawn. The patriarch of it all, Mr. Walter Stewart, then came out onto the lawn and surveyed his minions. Mr. Stewart ordered me into the house.

Henry Laines, the newlywed, had locked himself into one of the sons' rooms and was sinking into a Weird Depression. Mary Grace was collapsed in a Hysterical Fit. One of the sons was home from Harvard on vacation with a girl. The Harvard couple was passed out in a Drug Sordor on the living room couch. Another son, having just announced his engagement, had caused a group of Mississippi aunts and other relatives to embark on a screaming discussion of wedding details in the kitchen. In short, the scene was chaos, and I passed on, to see what might be happening down the street at the Colliers' house, where Mr. Collier was no doubt trying to bring order out of chaos.

••◦••

Mr. Collier was standing in the driveway doing two of his evening rituals at once — picking up shells in the gravel, and listening to the Baptist minister on a small portable TV.

Mr. Collier always tried to Pick Up Shells in the gravel, even though it would be impossible to ever completely get all the shells out of the gravel. I often pointed this out, but Mr. Collier would just smile dreamily and continue to slowly pick up shells with a faraway expression.

As for the Baptist minister, this was also an enigma. "Why does he do that?" I often asked Mrs. Collier. But she did not know.

"Why do you listen to that nut?" I often asked Mr. Collier, who was not a religious man. But he would just chuckle enigmatically and look at me fondly.

I have already told you what I have deduced, that the bottom secret of an eccentric is that he does not know why he does it, he just does it.

Once, Mr. Collier finally allowed that sometimes the Baptist minister used ancient Greek phrases, and then Mr. Collier would look them up. Ancient Greek phrases. Then Mr. Collier would look them up in his beloved Homer. Once I found him standing at his desk, watching the Baptist minister on the portable TV while listening to ancient Greek on a Walk-Man.

"What is the purpose of that?" I asked.

But of course, he did not know.

--⧓⧓⧓--

Claude was standing outside of the grocery store on the corner of Washington and Carondelet, giving money to some wino lunatic and then carrying his groceries down the street.

When Claude saw me, he bid his companion good-bye, and then I gave a lecture about why did he have to hang around with wino lunatics and racetrack habitués and other weird types of wrecks and make them into his dependents.

"Come on," he said quietly, in that gentle voice. "I'll work it out," he said. "Louise, you're a kick," he added, I don't know why. He looked at me and laughed.

This fellow had a light heart—or at least pretended to.

--⧓⧓⧓--

The next day at work I went to lunch with Earl, the born-again Christian, and Mr. LaSalle. Earl was the kind of person who, when you were with him at a restaurant, would start drawing his family tree on a napkin. To those not uninterested in Mississippi history, or in people who were nuts, or in the family history of nuts, this habit definitely had its points—except when Earl went too far and traced his forebears back to Louis XIV, King of France. But that only made him more of a nut, which was good.

Nuts made life worth living.

Since the glory days of the Sun King, however, Earl's family had fallen on harder times. His father was a notary in our firm—the King of Notaries, I called him. I think that was why they didn't fire Earl for preaching in the office—because his father was the King of Notaries. He was the oldest employee.

We went to lunch at the Sazerac Bar in the Roosevelt Hotel. It was a picturesque duo, Earl and Mr. LaSalle, two nuts—what could be better? The decor of the Sazerac Bar was like a miniature tropic republic, with gilt palm trees in pairs at intervals along the walls, dessert in the shape of swans, and black waiters in, appropriately, Louis XIV costumes with ruffles at the cuffs, a tropic grotesquerie.

Earl drew his family tree on a napkin and described his personal relationship with the Lord and the writhing torments of the fires of Hell.

Mr. LaSalle became quite sentimental after he drank a few beers, and sang "After the Ball Is Over" at top volume for a toast, causing a certain stunned silence in the bar.

They were off on a frolic of their own. That was the type of nuts they were.

—❦—

There was a cocktail party for the Russians. The Russians were involved in an admiralty case at the office. The office had a lot of admiralty work, often with foreign dignitaries. The partners circulated a memo saying that everyone should go to the cocktail party and should drink vodka to Be Polite to the Russians.

Mr. LaSalle gave his rendition of "I'm a Stranger in Paradise," which I thought was especially appropriate.

I had to go over to the Fifth Circuit Court of Appeals after the cocktail party to deliver something to the judge's office. The judge was playing pool with the clerks. The judge was a noble and illustrious one, and although his clerks came from Harvard and vied for the positions in his office, they played pool all day.

The judge was so smart that he only worked half days, but still got all the work done. Books have been written about his intelligence, his integrity, his industry—and to those for whom the law is a stern mistress, his name will be known without my saying it. But the books don't mention his pool-playing ability.

-→⋙⋘←-

It was Latin American Night in the Quarter, in Jackson Square, starting at eight o'clock. The time is gone when we were "the gateway to the Americas" and ships left our harbor daily for Havana with all the men wearing white suits. But all the men still wear white suits in New Orleans, on certain summer days.

There were bulbs strung up in Jackson Square among the lush green of the banana trees and the elephant ear, with small black children tap dancing to the Latin band. I met Claude at the Hilton Hotel, where he was smoking Tareytons and wearing a dark blue suit—distinguished, familiar, and dear. His dark hair was slicked straight back austerely. But he looked like a cross between a crackpot and a normal, conservative young man. You couldn't tell which would win out.

We went to a party on St. Claude Avenue, as it happened, across the Industrial Canal in Araby, at the corner of Desire. There was another Latin band and magnolia trees. After that, we ended up going to a party in the country through the Louisiana green. We went through the rows of sugarcane and pending hurricanes and all that which is strangely comforting.

I swear, when it comes to the place you are from, even the dirt looks different. For even the roots of the oak trees in Audubon Park make strange music to me, of my childhood in a town which is gentle to the bottom of its bones and which is far from peril.

Everyone was in the garden by the oaks, a collection of laconic young men in khaki suits who had conventional jobs downtown and were perfectly willing to sit in that garden until four in the morning, calmly and devotedly out on a binge. Among the venerable oaks and Spanish moss and the haze of the late afternoon, I was looking out at the tropic night from the slightly unintelligible elegance of the plantation style. I felt a loyalty to it, and to its refuge, its defeat.

We were at St. Louis Plantation in Placquemines, which is the heart of the remote, unknown South. There you see an unlikely glamour, pink antebellum mansions suddenly alone by the levee in their obscure grace almost as though it were a joke, a sort of sad one, though, as if the madcap Southerners had put one over on the world, to set these mansions at the edge of the world where there is no one near. Now there are huge oil distilleries and grain elevators along the River Road, which make it seem like Mars. But they, too, are hidden here at the edge of the levee and the rows of sugarcane, against an orange sky.

The halls of the plantation were mahogany, with huge four-poster beds and Audubon prints and cots on the attic floor and otherwise no furniture but threadbare elegance. This threadbare elegance meant more to me than any glittering metropolis and busy companies of men.

There was a house party on the glittering lake. We had a boating party on the lake. We went into the bayou to the Boguefalaya with dead tree trunks all black and twisted and cows standing in the water. We had boiled crabs and cantaloupes and tomatoes for dinner. Some people got plastered. Claude dropped his plate on his lap after some girl paid him a compliment. He dropped his entire plate, amid formal dead silence at the table. Then when he went to get another one and was returning across the lawn, while the whole table was watching him approach, he stepped on a can, which made a loud noise, and then tripped over it and nearly fell, while everyone watched his catastrophes.

--->≡≪--

"Louise, watch that boy in the street," said Claude while I was driving the car. "Honey, watch out, this is a one-way street," he said as I weaved my way in and out of the traffic, under the marvelous oaks, there in the late night down the Avenue. He kept telling me directions and cautions as though he were some kind of Frail Older Gentleman, the way he sometimes seemed as though he were about eighty, even though he was wild.

In truth, Claude was different and wise and older. He had an air of distraction, striding along beside me, as though he looked far down somewhere in the Quarter where I couldn't see.

In Napoleon House, with the crumbling walls, the "Hallelujah Chorus" was playing when we walked in, by the portraits of Napoleon brooding while his soldiers sack the Tuileries. The night was fairly balmy. No one was there. The waiter knew us. It was very pleasant. Until some got too drunk and threw their coats down in the gutter and had no cash and I had to stop the order for more champagne and became alarmed. But some decaying social conservatives in seersucker suits in the back room saved us and took care of the bill.

There was some sort of jazz revolution going on in Armstrong Park, formerly Congo Square, with black men in gold suits with sequins or dapper summer whites. A black man in a white suit came across the lagoon in a pirogue, standing up and playing a mournful trumpet solo in the night, and then he landed over at the Gospel Tent. There were rickety old black men in pink ruffled suits with jazz umbrellas, dancing for the crowd—and you felt that if at least you were near to people like that, then maybe you were not weak, if you could even be near to such as them.

Summer whites, green gardens, Mississippi, white summer suits and seersucker suits, those were the sights. In the Garden District, Claude stopped and pointed out the jasmine and the cicadas in the night. That was his innocence to me. He had the sweetness of the town itself and broke my heart completely into a million pieces on the floor, as he himself would say, for he touched my heart, to such degree, that I had to steel myself, or my heart would break, like his, into a million pieces on the floor. For in Claude Collier I saw my very youth, a fateful green garden, parades on the Avenue, an orchestra on a bandstand, my youth in New Orleans.

I knew him so well that I knew him in my bones, and I saw, among other things, that in him. But at the end of the night what I did not see was that Claude sat with a bottle and was unable to lay his head down, went back out dancing until dawn, back to the party on St. Claude and Desire, and got in a minor car wreck on the bridge over the Industrial Canal on the way home, and had to go to Night Court in Araby.

But there he could talk to his friends, no doubt, in Central Lock-Up.

-->∋≡€--

Youthful folly is a thing which we had a great deal of in New Orleans. It is a thing which has its season, and its season is youth. I was surprised when I came back from college in the East to see how long it pended with some people I knew. But I still felt there was a season for it and that we were still in it. If it went on too long—that would separate me from those who did it too long. Nor do I know how you can tell someone to be sensible—simply, to be sensible.

I left New Orleans when I was young, to go to college in the East. But I came back immediately after, and spent many palmy days there. The Defeat and Humiliation of the South is a true thing. Among the Yankees I have known, I only met one who had the grace to apologize to me about the War. So as peoples throughout history have been chastened and put down, I retreated in Dignity and Pride back to New Orleans.

As an obscure provincial who was once in New York, I can say that my experience in New York was not a pretty one. I went on dates with New York boys who were writers and journalists who were total strangers who were intellectuals. It was mentally exhausting. I thought of my absent beloved, who was wise in the heart, who did not talk like them. But he, who had his own money, and did not appear to have ambition, was sweltering in the dream of his native town.

-->∋≡€--

Claude labored without a clear conscience—or, at least, so it seemed to him. It had nothing to do with whether or not he really was base, which he was not. It had only to do with that he suspected himself to be. You might call it humility or self-effacement or perspective, but it is really nothing but a type of torture, and it held Claude back.

He had an exaggerated view of his own insignificance. He saw himself as an inconsequential person of no consequence walking down the Street of Life.

This view may be fair enough, but there is also something wrong in it, preventing one from action.

Claude felt that he had something to atone for, but the poor fellow did not know what it was. He felt that if he hated himself there must be some sound reason for it.

→⟩※⟨←

My brother, Capability Brown, named for the English architect, was my closest relative in New Orleans. The story is told, at least of Cap Brown, that he got the name because he would look at a site and say, "Hmmm. Yes. That has capability."

I tell this story because in a way it is what I saw in Claude.

I was brought up by my aunts in New Orleans. My aunts were from Baltimore, Mississippi, where I was born. When I was one year old, my mother took me and Cap and parked us in New Orleans with her three sisters, my aunts—a shady business. So I grew up with my aunts, who spent long afternoons talking about how nice the porters on the trains—always named George—used to be.

My aunts and I received dividend checks from companies like Louisiana Rice Milling Co. and Mid-South Utilities.

We were the beneficiaries of a family fortune made in Mississippi in the lumber business and administered by the trustees.

We never talked about it.

It gave me Moral Qualms, however.

Mr. Collier was one of the trustees. At times, I went to his office, and he would explain the fluctuations of the lumber business being run by apathetic, rum-soaked members of my mother's family in Mississippi. But in an atmosphere of opera and rhapsodes, Mr. Collier gave me the checks in such a mild spirit of kindness and simplicity that I didn't have the heart to discuss my Existential Crises with him. He sat at his desk in his dilapidated seersucker suit, opera in the air, and looked after the affairs of his many clients.

Mr. Collier loved habit and routine, which took away his possible Existential Crises.

Every day at three, for instance, he would go to the barber shop in the basement of the Louisiana Bank Building and have his shoes shined. As he was famous for doing this, he was often accosted by his clients or old friends while he was having his shoes shined.

You didn't have to knock on the door at Mr. Collier's office; you just walked in. And if he was not there, you could find him in the basement of the Louisiana Bank Building, having his shoes shined.

Otherwise you could be sure to find him at noon in The Pearl, having a dozen oysters. These were his daily rituals, which he had practiced faithfully for forty years. It was what he called celebrating the mundane.

He attached himself to his duty and, during the interstices of time, he innocently performed his rigid daily rituals, without which he would certainly have Fallen Apart.

As for my aunts, they were another story. They would have screaming discussions all afternoon about the old days in their Mississippi drawls.

--›☒‹--

There was a ceremony for Mr. Collier in Audubon Park, where they were dedicating a plaque to him.

It poured rain throughout. We all tramped through the rain to the statue of Audubon, where they had the dedication.

He who ennobled life and by his deeds and service hath won remembrance among men.

I looked at the inscription in the pouring rain, among the lush green, the palmetto garden by the statue slashing against the plaque in the tropic rain. Twenty years later, I stood in the same spot on a rainy, rainy day and regarded again the same commemoration to whom I consider as my father, my beloved father. A sudden happiness, a gust of happiness, swept through my house, my life, just as, at the time, a gust of hope swept through me when I was with them then, and knew that they were kind. Mr. Collier sat on a bench watching the dedication, in the pouring rain, with his son Saint beside him.

The men were in white linen suits and mopping their brows with white handkerchiefs in the heat. The orchestra was just finishing up, grouped on the bandstand in white suits against the unending green, in the dark shade. A couple of people in the orchestra opened up black umbrellas and started traipsing toward the street.

⇥⇤

That night I was at the Colliers' house, watching Saint. No one else was home except for Byron. Saint was standing on the balcony, pretending to strangle himself, for the benefit of Byron, below. Saint staggered melodramatically toward the railing. Byron stood below, writhing in hilarity. Then Saint hooked himself halfway over the balcony, lunging with his torso embedded in the railing, screaming.

"Pirates! The ship! Abandon ship!" Saint screamed in a strangled shriek. Then he changed his position and crawled completely over the railing, getting ready to let himself down and land on a patch of grass under the balcony.

He dropped.

"Jesus, Mercy, Lord," said Byron quietly, awestruck.

Saint was crumpled on the patch of grass, howling—he had fallen on his arm in a twisted position. I went and scooped him up.

"We better take him to the Emergency Room," I said to Byron. "I think he broke his arm. Come on, let's go. We're going to the hospital."

Byron, regaining the use of his senses, tried to convince me to let him drive us in his car.

"I could drive," he pleaded. "I could drive, Louise."

Saint, for some reason, stopped crying. He was a little stoic, lying in my arms. Maybe the nerves in his arm had gone dead.

"Does it still hurt?" I ventured.

He assented, with dignity.

As it is said, the boy is the man in miniature, and in that moment Saint was like his brother, with his unpretentious dignity—even at five years old. I had a pint-sized little genius on my hands, one with a unique noble air.

"It's probably just sprained," he said, looking studiously at his arm.

I pointed out to Byron that we all three couldn't possibly fit in his car, and that even if we could, we would probably get thrown off the road, and no matter how furiously he pedaled down Prytania Street in his little car, it would not work out.

I laid Saint down in the back seat of Claude's green VW, which was parked in front of the house. Byron sat in front with his head craned around staring at the victim.

⸻

The victim gallantly displayed light-heartedness in adversity. They put a small cast on his arm. The cast went from his wrist to several inches below his elbow, like a sweat band for tennis, and received many Latin salutations and ancient Greek characters from Mr. Collier later that evening. The nurses billed and cooed and talked about how adorable Saint was. Saint looked back at them with a strangely knowing though shy stare, older than his years. He had the tentative strength of someone just recovering from a nervous breakdown, and this quality was unusual in one so young.

We had to stop several times so Saint could drink about twenty Cokes with unquenchable fervor, on the way home from the hospital. Byron too had trouble extinguishing a craving thirst for carbonation. It restored them to their customary pitch of frenzy.

⸻

Wednesday night, Claude was playing football with Saint in the garden. Then he went over to a bar and started drinking White Russians, one after the other.

This was a bar that had an atmosphere that had been arrested in 1965. Everyone in it wore loafers, silly sports hats, alligator shirts, and bright pastel-colored pants. The jukebox played dated songs from a specific era whose moment has definitely passed.

Later, Claude went home and worked on his betting plots late into the night, until he lay down in bed and could feel his heart rattling within him, and every time the steamboats on the river blew their fog horns, it caused a sort of convulsion of Claude's poor graceful frame.

He could not sleep well, and suffered trouble in his heart.

⸻

His telephone started ringing at seven in the morning. It rang and rang. A rude, dream-like awakening, somehow calm, it roused him from his stupor, and he listened on the wire.

It was his father—there had been an accident—his father told him on the line. Then Claude was unearthly calm and efficient in his exhaustion, though reckless in his blue eyes, pulling on a suit and driving downtown to the hospital.

It had happened in the night, or actually in the small hours of the morning. Saint was up, going to the bathroom, to get a glass of water, or possibly to investigate the house on some Mission of Adventure. In his intrepid, reckless way, more exaggerated than usual with a boy of five, he went out on the balcony to see the garden in the night.

It was night, dark, and no one was there. Saint looked at a nearby magnolia tree, no doubt considering some danger-fraught climbing expedition. He climbed to the top of the railing, swaying bravely toward the magnolia tree, and he caught his pajamas in the grillework. The cuff of his pants tore away as he wavered, losing his balance, and he fell to the side of the balcony, onto some decaying bricks in the garden, making a muffled sound—and he was not found until morning, by his father, with a little pool of coagulating blood around his blond head. The sight did not undo Mr. Collier, or sink into his brain, until some months later than that.

─⟩⊞⟨─

Claude Collier woke up in the morning with his fists clenched. He had taken his phone off the hook. He stayed up late into the night—just to drink and be tormented, and then fall into a stupor. I thought of many things he would require now, austerity and wrath. I thought he had better try to get some philosophical indifference to the world. But wrath was not in his nature, and neither austerity, and it would be a hard road for Claude.

Everyone says time heals, but he did not see it that way. His grief was the same to him as knowing the multiplication tables—a knowledge he could never deny, whose factuality could never abate. Everything about it would always be like some flat, enduring set of facts often referred to in life. It is not outlandish to think of the many nights he would lie in his bed, years and years later than this, and be stricken with the worst grief he ever knew. In other things, Claude didn't grieve. He was one who never looked on the bad side. But late at night he would lie in his bed and say aloud the name, Saint. And try to dream of that boy, picture the years of his childhood, and get to sleep at last by this method. But he was uncomprehending, incredulous.

It was the strangest, most unlawful thing Claude Collier ever knew.

❖

Claude pasted up on his icebox those pathetic grade-school photographs of his brother, the kind where the child is wearing a black string tie as though he were a Texan. "The little angel," he said, did this, did that, the angel, the saint. He counted the minutes in a day, and considered it an arduous trial to live from one minute to the next. The only answer seemed to be to tear down his illusions, change his life. "Error is all in the not done, all in the diffidence that faltered."

He got out of bed at night, in the nameless hour, and listened to opera, the volume at full blast. He had never liked opera—now he listened to it all the time, as though it might stave off something inconsolable.

During the day, he drove to the tennis courts and played opera at full volume on the tape deck in his green VW. He sat staring at the tennis courts, in the dark greenness of the city, St. Charles Avenue implausibly gentle and grand as it stretched down past view. There he sat, with opera blaring by the tennis courts, oblivious and intent.

He drank rum and Cokes in the Tulane bar by the tennis courts until he was too drunk to drive home; then he drove home.

He went to Henry Laines' house; Henry Laines tried to console him. Henry called him up all the time. "Why don't you take the streetcar up here?" Henry would say with his urbane accent.

In his rooms, Henry hung ominous paintings of Mardi Gras balls, where the queens and debutantes had insanely wide smiles and skeletal frames, holding their scepters rigid in the air. Bland men in tuxedos stood grouped around them, smiling weakly. This was Henry's plea for satire.

Then he would call me up. "Tell Claude to come over. Tell him to take the streetcar up here."

But they just ended up getting into fights. Henry was wrathful and raving—that was his temperament—and lost his patience with Claude, who was always calm. Claude would never raise a temper—as he proceeded through life with his mild demeanor, protecting others, holding them together, while they attached themselves to him and his steady solicitude. They would be falling apart, but he wouldn't be, or at least would not show himself to be. No one knew how to help him, who had always helped so many others; and he did not even seem to know that he was much beloved by many. He had a dry feeling. He would take a drink to try to get some feeling back, to try to get insights or emotions, and to rouse him from his daze.

"I have a headache. Let me get a drink," Claude said, and left to go back to his car and turn on opera at full blast as he drove down the boulevards. The church bells rang in the fading afternoon light and could be heard up and down St. Charles Avenue.

It was his way to claim that he had never known despair, but I believe he had, even before this. I think it followed him down the green boulevards, and was his frequent companion. It told him that his desires were futile and that it is futile to hope or expect things, that hope is a tinsel thing which vainly flaps its tinsel wing, and told Claude therefore to be strong, alone.

"Repair it by flight," said St. Augustine. But no man can Escape Himself.

→►☰◄→

His sleeping habits had never been good. He went to bed late and often rose early, but always his bed was a jail, a chore, an unpleasant duty, and he didn't fall asleep until three or four. He lamented always the same thing—the waste—and woke up with regret for it again in the very morning.

The theme was that he hated himself too much to inflict himself on anyone in New Orleans. You might say he felt he owed his town more than he could pay. So then why not a city full of strangers, for its pleasant anonymity and Intoxicating Streets. So then why not New York?

"Louise," Claude said aloud, alone in his room.

Then one day he boarded a train for New York and "climbed the sharp hill that led to all the years ahead."

❧❦❧

I was standing on a balcony of the funeral home, which was on St. Charles Avenue. It was an elegant parade of gray and dark blue limousines going stark and ruthless, in funereal pomp, down the Avenue, and it seemed like everyone I knew was either drunk or in a fight with someone or had gotten in near-fatal car wrecks.

The azaleas were out. It was the last day of April, when the tropic spring gives a harsh, bright color to things. Claude stood in a trance at the cemetery; it was after the funeral. He was the last one to leave the grave. There were not so many trees at the cemetery, and so it was not as gentle there, not so green, as it usually was in that town. Everything looked stark. The graves are above ground in New Orleans, with whitewashed vaults in the heat.

I stood waiting for Claude. Then he turned and came over to me. As though he had not seen me before, he came rashly over and grabbed me. It seemed he would never let go.

The cemetery, which was in Metairie, had put up a large green-and-white striped tent over the Colliers' plot, with deck chairs underneath it lined up in rows, as gay as though for a wedding reception. Though really it was done for respite from the heat.

Across the road from the cemetery there was a very large, dazzling green lawn. I was looking at it from our embrace, when it seemed Claude would never let go — and it seemed to me that the thing had been planned long ago. A gust of breeze swept past in the luminous twilight while I looked at that ravishing lawn, in his rash embrace, and it seemed he would never let me go.

I said nothing. The most incalculably good thing I could think of to say was nothing. Saint was "like memory of music fled" — in his brother's heart, and I could not presume to trespass there.

"Affection is never wasted," said the priest, quoting from the

Bible. "Angels can fly for they take themselves lightly," the priest said.

That was like Claude, who did not think of himself, and who deprecated himself, and who, on the whole, at least formerly, was always making jokes. He ordinarily behaved with gallant levity, but he was not light-hearted in this adversity.

—>❦<—

There is a day I remember from somewhere that reminded me of Claude. I remember it on a day in one's extreme youth, a day that is vaguely athletic and the air so crisp in the fall as to be almost melancholic. There are a lot of leaves on the lawn and a football game somewhere—it could be Cambridge, Massachusetts—light filters into a white-painted room, and Claude is drinking gin, and he is ardently happy. It is a paltry thing, but I remember that day.

I had heard a lot of stories, when I was up North at college, about Claude's life—something about Mary Grace, some binges, disasters, accidents, and worse things—a catastrophe-ridden life, just like the life of his brother Saint. Claude was wild, but ardor is a profoundly great quality that only the strong can have as frequently as he did. In such a way, he got to know the world, and he acquired his air of humanity.

For myself, different from him as is the day from the night, the moth from the star, there is a different devotion. For myself, I remember a certain day on a green German lake, and it was a place out of time, with a bandstand and chairs set in rows—Baden-Baden, a mysterious town of German renown, with swans on the green lake. There was a concert of Albinoni, a noble lament, for time immemorial. It commemorated a way to live your life. It was something to hold up, as a guide. But no one can describe the dignity of music, because it is, like the great things in life, not spoken. But there on the green German lake it seemed it was the desire for love in all men that alone brought philosophical anguish. From this desire, none are exempt. The bravest are the least exempt.

Mr. Collier at the grave reminded me of the Lido in Venice, the most philosophical place that I have ever seen, with its gloomy gaiety and ruined grandeur, the green water stretching mildly out in an expanse past view. There was a philosophical indifference about the place, but the "sad still music of humanity" hung in the air, from centuries long past.

I have known three great men and Mr. Collier was among them. I will not soon forget that gallant, forlorn group, standing there in the green beauty of the South.

⟶⟩⊞⟨⟵

At his house, after the funeral, Claude acted pretty strange. He made a lot of weirdo jokes. He drank. He made more jokes than usual.

It was funny, in an uneasy sort of way, that the funeral reminded me of Henry Laines' wedding. Both occurred in a languid winter, toward a tropic spring—the wedding at eighty degrees, then cooler on the day of the funeral, seventy degrees on the last day of April. At the wedding, everyone waltzed around in anterooms, with the principals in dignified black—a scene not too wildly unlike the Colliers' house after the funeral.

As at Henry's wedding, Claude again felt it his duty to fix all the drinks and chain-smoke Tareytons, while people loitered at the iron gate in the humidity and intermittent light rain and dark green of the Garden District, a small crowd of people with the women in beige clothes.

⟶⟩⊞⟨⟵

When Saint was born, Mr. and Mrs. Walter Stewart had gone to the hospital to sit with Mr. Collier while he waited. It was a spectacular childbirth because Mrs. Collier was fifty at the time and Mr. Collier was fifty-seven. He especially was thoroughly nervous to be a father again at that age, uncertain that he would be able to raise a child properly. Mrs. Stewart had brought a little suitcase containing lemons, a bottle of Scotch, plastic glasses, martini shakers, etc. Things were not wholly different at his death, at the house that day, in the dark mahogany rooms like a conservatory with so many flowers.

Mr. Stewart delivered a tirade to Claude, which began, "Son, your grandfather was the finest..."

Claude listened politely, with his eyes cast down.

"Your father was first in his class at the law school. Your grandfather ... Finest law firm in ... Claude, why don't you want to go to law school?"

Mrs. Stewart was vivacious and incoherent and talked for a very long time about how to cook fish. Her mother-in-law stood in the hall and put her hands on my shoulders and said, with an important, searching air, "Louise, I am going to be eighty-four this spring, and you know, dear, I am ancient." She lowered her eyes in a coquettish gesture and, with a theatricality reminiscent of her son, she went on, "There is one thing I would like to know before going to my reward. I want to know one thing, and I want to *know* it." She paused. "Why are the young people of today so unkempt?"

I laughed nervously.

"Tell me about your beaux, Louise," she said.

I seemed to remember hearing this conversation before.

"I remember all of my old beaux," said Mrs. Stewart. "None of them ever had a greater plight than to see that I behaved. I used to wear a size four, you know. When I was fifteen years old," she continued, "Teague Smith made me a proposal of marriage. He was a thirty-five-year-old man at the time. Well, my brother prevented the marriage—and it was not the only engagement of mine that he broke. As you know, no man had a greater plight than to fall into my path when I was fifteen years old. I remember the night Teague Smith came to the door with the ring—I remember it vividly. I have many secrets, you know. But I married Monroe Stewart, Sr.," she went on, "and Monroe Stewart, Sr., was my husband for thirty-seven years."

Mr. Collier came in and was listening attentively, his eyes vague, in a state of high, almost perfect contentment to hear the eloquence of the debutante—even at eighty-four years old. She had a streak of native, wrathful intelligence which she cleverly disguised with coquetry. It was a curious but spellbinding mixture.

→≻≋≺←

In the kitchen, Claude was ripping apart a piece of chicken with his hands, staring morosely at his mother. She, in turn, stood staring back at him.

"Claude, couldn't you just use a plate?" Mrs. Collier said finally.

"No, Mother, I could not use a plate. I could not use a fork. I must eat with my bare hands."

"Where are your manners?" Mrs. Collier said. "We raised you, we taught you manners."

"I have no manners," Claude said. He went to the stove and lifted the cover of a large pot.

"Lima beans," he said morosely. "I can't believe it. You and Mrs. Stewart making lima beans all afternoon, just sitting around making lima beans. I mean, who really likes lima beans? Who really likes them? No one does. I hate lima beans. No one really likes lima beans."

"Lower your voice," Mrs. Collier said.

"Was I talking loud? I'm sorry. I'm falling apart," Claude said.

"You were screaming," said Mrs. Collier.

"Just because they were making lima beans," I interjected, "it isn't exactly a reflection on anything. It doesn't mean some huge thing."

"Yes, it does," Claude said. "It means some huge thing. Like that dress you're wearing. It means some huge thing."

"Like what?"

"Like that I—" He stopped. "Lima beans," he continued. "It's just kind of disgusting," he trailed off.

--)BC--

He walked dejectedly over to the icebox and began rummaging around in the freezer. Finally locating his beloved Acqua-Pac, Claude attached it to his head. Then he took off his shoes and started asking everyone in the kitchen for drink orders. The pointy blue sunglasses of Acqua-Pac made him look like a visitor from another planet.

"Please, Darling," said Mrs. Collier. "Not that."

"What?" Claude said.

"That headpiece. Please, Darling, please, get a grip on yourself."

--)BC--

"Claude, you have to learn how to express anger," said Mrs. Collier. "You don't express anger. Do you agree with that?"

"I agree with Louise, whatever she says," Claude said.

Tom, the young debauchee, beckoned me outside at the gate. He was wearing his Walk-Man with his black suit.

"Why don't you take him to the bamboo grove?" he said.

"What's that? The bamboo grove?"

"You remember."

"Oh, yes, I remember—at the wedding."

⟶⟩⟨⟵

"I saw my aunts this morning," I said to Claude, "They send you their best."

"Really? What did they say?"

"They said to send you their best."

"And then what did you say?"

"I said I will."

"And then what did they say?"

"They said good, please do."

"And then what did you say?"

"I said fine."

"And then what did they say?"

"Oh, God, quit it, Claude."

⟶⟩⟨⟵

"Did you have breakfast at your aunts' this morning?" Claude said.

"Yes."

"What did you have?"

"I had scrambled eggs."

He fell silent, and started breaking chicken bones into an ashtray.

"Did I tell you my brother's fish died?" Claude said. "Wait, I want Mrs. Stewart to hear about this. Where is she? Mrs. Stewart," he called out, "did I tell you my brother's fish died?"

"Why . . . I'm sorry to hear that, Claude," said Mrs. Stewart the elder, eyeing Mrs. Collier and me questioningly.

"Oh, I didn't tell you? Its eyeball fell out."

"Please don't tell that story again, Claude," said Mrs. Collier.

"No, I better tell. Its eyeball got caught in the siphon leading from the fish tank out through the window and the fish was dead and then his eyeball came out. So I wrapped it up—the fish, not the eyeball—and put it outside in the trash can and then the cat ate it," he said in a monotone.

"Claude, please," said Mrs. Collier.

Mrs. Stewart offered a timid smile.

-⫸⫷-

Mary Grace walked into the kitchen rather unsteady on her feet.

"Can I get you a drink, Mary Grace?" said Claude.

"Thank you, Claude. How are you feeling?"

"Oh, not so hot—I have a cold," he said, and looked at her expectantly. "Get it? Not so *hot*, I have a *cold*?" Then he laughed maniacally.

She was standing vaguely behind him while he fixed her drink—green Chartreuse in a shot glass with Louisiana red pepper—don't ask me why—and she was looking across at me.

"I love your hair," she called out to me.

"Thanks."

She walked over to me and threw herself down into a chair, stared at me penetratingly for about five deeply ruminative minutes, and then finally said, "What kind of hairdo does your mother have?"—as though the answer to this question was going to give her the key to my character. Even though I didn't say anything, she was gripped by a torrent of maudlin affection.

"Louise, I just want to tell you something: I love you. I just think you're so sweet. I love you. You're so funny. You're such a scream. Well, I had a Bloody Mary at my mother's house this morning at breakfast, and then I had two Grand Marniers after lunch at the restaurant, I mean, I had two Bloody—but I mean, I just love you. Do you know what I mean? I really love you."

"I love you, too," I said.

She leaned over to me confidentially and said in a low tone, "I was out of town when this happened. I couldn't believe it. I had to come back in last night. It reminds me of the time Henry told me he wished I would cut all my hair off."

Oh, my God, I thought, what does she mean by that? The funeral reminds her of the time Henry told her to cut all her hair off? What could she possibly mean by that?

Then she got on the subject of marriage. She told me that sleeping with Henry was like sleeping with World War II. Then she got on the subject of shoes.

"I always wear a high heel. I'm fashion conscious. I mean, I follow fashion. Henry told me he wished I would wear flat shoes—so I said, Henry, if you want a girl who wears flat shoes, then let's just get a divorce. Because I'll always wear a high heel. That's all there is to it, I'll always wear a high heel."

I coughed and laughed at the same time, not knowing exactly what to say, and practically strangled myself. To further the conversation, I said, "I think Henry looks great."

"So do a lot of homosexuals," she said, and then burst into hysterics.

Oh, my God, what does she mean by that? I thought.

"Dawlin, come over here," she called out to Claude. "Wait—did you hear this cute thing I just said?"

She's having some kind of attack, I thought. She's having some kind of breakdown, I thought, as she weaved her way over to Claude. I went out into the garden to brood.

→⊰⊱←

Claude was still sitting in the kitchen, fixing drinks for whoever came in and striking up weird conversations with them. He was talking to the undertaker.

It happened that the undertaker was a darkly glamorous twenty-nine-year-old man born in Paris. The funeral home was the family business, generations-old, elaborate and sumptuous, and the city's oldest, a society funeral home. They were a society family. Claude had beckoned the undertaker into the kitchen, saying he wanted to "talk shop." Then he asked the undertaker what kind of funeral he would like to have himself, after seeing so many other people's funerals, and what kind of burial he would like to have. The glamorous undertaker said, "I would like to be exploded."

"You mean, exploded, like with dynamite, at the funeral?" said Claude.

"Yes."

This was Claude's kind of person.

I went back into the garden to brood. I absented myself with some frequency that day in order to go off and brood.

—)▩(—

I overheard Mr. Stewart saying something to Mr. Collier. I heard Mr. Stewart say, "Louis Collier, I have one thing to say to you. When you were called to the bench, I knew that justice would begin to be served. I may have taken a drink or two, but it's fifty years that I've been with you and known that this was true: Louis Collier, a finer soul than you never breathed. A finer soul never walked the earth. I admire you more than anyone I've ever known. Please allow me to say that my admiration for you exceeds all the proprieties and knows no bounds."

Mr. Collier patted him on the back, his mind preoccupied with other things.

"You perjure yourself, old man," Mr. Collier said mildly, gently.

Then I heard Mr. Stewart say, "Saint," as he sometimes called Mr. Collier, "I'll never forget this day. You know I love you, Saint."

Mr. Collier went into his friend's arms.

"It's not often that a man has to bury his son," said Mr. Collier.

—)▩(—

"Life's too short to be unhappy," said Mr. Stewart to Claude. "I don't have the answers, son," he added.

Claude was sitting with Mr. Stewart in the kitchen. Many regarded Mr. Walter Stewart as one of the great bores living, but Claude Collier and his father both found him profoundly interesting. Mr. Stewart was a member of Mr. Collier's club, where he was affectionately known as the Club Bore.

Mr. Stewart and Claude were getting into a discussion of taxes. Mr. Stewart, named by Mr. Collier, was Claude's lawyer. They sometimes discussed his circumstances. Mr. Stewart took a dim view of them.

"I'll see you in Atlanta, son," said Mr. Stewart darkly.

"How's that, Walter?"

"There's a federal penitentiary in Atlanta, son. It's where you go when you don't pay your taxes."

-->⊞<--

Our old friend Byron—who did not understand what had happened
—raced across the room and stopped between Mrs. Legendre's legs,
emitting a loud screech meant to simulate the abrupt stop of a
racing car.

"Why don't you go out and play in some traffic?" said Mrs.
Legendre in her crestfallen, gravel-voiced monotone, looking down
at the small black figure pretending to be a car.

-->⊞<--

Claude was lying on his bed in his room with his hands folded on
his chest as people in their coffins do, with his eyes closed and the
record player blaring wild sexy saxophone music that was the
instrumental episode from "Smoke Gets in Your Eyes," which he
had been playing millions of times each day for the past week.
When it came to the refrain, Claude would scream along with the
music in an ascending sort of scream of passion.

He was wearing an old plaid bathrobe over his suit.

In a corner of the living room, outside, there was a camp of
Claude's special admirers—wino lunatics, dissipated businessmen,
crooked politicians, demented young lawyers, and odd-looking
men with black-and-white checkered sports jackets and garish
avocado-colored shirts, with hacking coughs.

"Thank God, you're all right," he said when I walked in. "I was
worried. How are you, really? Are you tired? Are you hungry? Do
you want a glass of water?"

His face looked sort of sallow, almost a type of green. I looked
at his old plaid bathrobe and pale ankles and pathetic bedroom
slippers and a wave swept over me and I knew—he was the only
person I had ever loved.

"You're so young, you're so young," he said wildly. "But you're
old enough for this," he said and looked at me. He said it in such a
worldly, even jaded way, as though suave of him, in a swift and
immediate moment. He smelled like a fall day in Boston, so sweet
it almost made me cry. His kisses were like conducting conversations with angels in Heaven.

He started making compliments, wild compliments, and then he started complimenting the sheets, the wallpaper, the furniture, after complimenting me. Then we lapsed into a state that was like a dark bedroom with the air-conditioning on high that you lay in when you were very young, like some old old times of heaven with someone, as though we had been this way since we were very young, though we had not, on the contrary, for it was sudden.

--⊃▓⊂--

There was this blaringly loud old-time saxophone music blaring through the house. In the crowd were Eli and Peter Stewart and their large brothers and their even larger father, their five hysterical, crackpot sisters with their good-old-boy husbands and screaming children, and other members of society, the fifty-year-olds looking stately and handsome, for life had been kind to them, and they to it, though there were some, like Mr. Legendre, with too florid jowls and a satyr-like air.

That was Society, and then there was the Fringe Society—the camp of wino lunatics, debauchees, and Wakamba Club habitués that made up Claude's special circles.

"See that woman?" said Claude to everyone, pointing at me. "She's my heart. I love her legs, I love her face, I love everything about her. She's my heart," he said.

A row of toothless, grinning old men sitting in the camp of wino lunatics smiled approvingly and one winked at me.

--⊃▓⊂--

Claude and I went to the bamboo grove. We went to the broom closet.

He looked at me intently, and there came a point when I looked into his face and could see his soul, of what he was made, the caliber of stuff that he was made of—the spark in him, or the essential quality, came clear in his face at that moment. Gentle and uncorrupt, essentially kind—and brainy, I swear, despite everything, despite his Southern inscrutability, his Southern good-old-boy aspects, which, after all, were many.

"Do I have a chance with you?" Claude said to me. "Love is like a garden," he said. "It starts out all scrappy and puny, but then you nurture it and then it blooms. It takes about fifty years, like anything else, but finally it blooms."

"Then when we are about eighty we'll be in ecstasy," I said.

—)⊞⦅—

A group of happy-go-lucky politicians, representatives from the mayor's office, were socializing at the bar. Mr. Collier was influential in the mayor's campaigns. The mayor came to the Colliers' house that day as well. He started leering at Mrs. Legendre. She was asking him about his recent trip to Europe.

"The parties were wonderful—that's why I'm mayor," he said incoherently.

"That kid doesn't have all his marbles," Mrs. Legendre whispered to me, regarding the mayor.

—)⊞⦅—

"That child was adorable," said Mrs. Stewart.

"He loves you so dearly," whispered Mrs. Collier. "I know he loves you dearly."

Everyone was leaving.

Mr. Collier went into the kitchen and sat down with Claude. He lit a cigar. His eyes were focused above Claude's head. Then he looked at him sedately. He puffed expansively on his cigar.

"Take things with a brave face. Never pity yourself. Three-fourths of all sorrow is self-pity. You must realize the inconsequence of your sorrows in the perspective of time.

"Secondly, you must pursue a course to its end. If you do, you'll succeed in it, I don't care what it is. This is what distinguishes a strong soul from a weak one, to persevere.

"Thirdly, put others above yourself. I've always told you to be kind. People will rely on you in life and you must protect them. Sometimes you must lie—to shield them. It is only a white lie. It's what is known as a white lie."

Mr. Collier puffed on his cigar.

"The last thing I want to tell you is open your heart, open your heart. 'The great secret of morals is love.' But you are probably one person I don't need to tell that to, Claude," he added admiringly, and was proud. "I think you have been able to open your heart more than I have been able to open mine," he said with his characteristic self-effacement.

They were silent for quite some time. Mr. Collier looked off into the garden. Claude shredded matchbooks and pierced holes in cigarette packages with a fountain pen. He drank two gin and tonics, but Mr. Collier did not seem to notice. They sat in their black suits, both with the same blue eyes, deep in affection, but stoic.

Finally Claude said, "I'm just longing for something there's no possible way I can get back." He cast his eyes down.

"Longing is built into the constitution of the mind," replied his father calmly.

"Do you have longings, sir?"

"Yes, I have infinite longing. The longings of a sixty-two-year-old man are infinite."

"I just have to get away for a while," said Claude.

His father said, "I planned for your brother and now it will be added to your property. This is your inheritance from him."

He handed him a piece of paper, many times folded, which he extracted from his inside breast pocket. "In the event of my death, I leave my property to my brother, St. Claude Collier," it read. It was signed by the trustee. "I set this aside for my little boy. Your great-aunt made over her further property in Mississippi, which was in the New Levee Trend, together with her property at Dauphin Island, where they also discovered oil."

Claude had his stricken expression.

"This makes it more than I expected because I had not sold the lease for the New Levee Well when I set this aside. You'll have to take care of that. As we had planned for you to take care of him, so you should take care of this, and take charge of your affairs. You'll have to continue with this as we planned, but under the circumstances, you'll have to realize—reconcile yourself to your advantages. You are lucky that you don't have to turn your hand to profit. You can follow your interests. Be mindful of your blessings. You have already paid a price for your advantages, I see. It is a man's duty to be happy. Life is uncertain, but what one longs for eventually comes to one. I don't have much religion, yet there are times when I—may God grant you what your heart desires, Son."

—)⊞€—

The idler's lot is a sad one. You would not want it yourself. Mr. Collier taught by example, not by directive. He did not give Claude guidance. The things he said at the funeral were the most guidance he had ever spoken. Claude had a subtle duty, but there was his aimlessness at the nerve. He was aimless at his core, as you may have observed. In this atmosphere you may understandably complain of a lack of plot or design, but that is the plot, that is the crisis—the crisis of youth and aimlessness.

He who is known as a ne'er-do-well, sometimes known as an underachiever, sometimes makes a sudden route to genius. An underachiever is someone who does not have ambition, and a ne'er-do-well is someone who can be found at the bar in the Lafayette Hotel at four in the morning on a weeknight, and both of those descriptions fit Claude Collier. But he later proved to have further attributes.

—)⊞€—

I walked out in the garden toward dark. Its beauty was remarkable. All the visitors had left. Claude's black suit stood out against all the dark green of the garden, as I went across to meet him.

"Now it is nothing except in my memory," he said. "I don't want it to be just in my memory. I don't want to forget."

He stood with his hands in his pockets.

"I wonder what is the matter with me," he said, "I can do nothing."

I thought that his cares would steal away, that they would "fold their tents like the Arabs, and as silently, steal away"—I beseeched them—steal away.

—)⊞€—

In the days after the funeral, it was sultry and everything was overgrown. In the evening, the blasts of the tropic spring swept through gardens and windows. Joggers with disco headphones ran down St. Charles Avenue. Small black children sang disco songs in languid unison while riding around on their bikes. We socialized in the garden, by the magnolia trees.

We were often in Henry Laines' garden, but Henry was mad. Henry was the type of person who goes into great rages. His specialty was getting mad at people and then going off by himself, leaving them alone at his house. He would get mad at them for small, tiny reasons, or else for things they had said six years ago, which would suddenly occur to him. Henry was the type of person who had enemies. He, in turn, cherished Lurid Animosities for his enemies. Yet he was uncharacteristically calm and tender when he shook Claude's hand at the gate. But then he left Claude and me in his garden while he went off by himself to think about why he was mad at Mary Grace.

His next-door neighbor, a person named Mel, wandered in through the gate. Mel was a Northerner, from Vermont, who spent his time fighting with Henry. Mel was a high-strung person, the type who would come bounding into your apartment and start rifling through drawers, while striking up arguments about politics. He was, in fact, not unlike Henry Laines, so they made a great pair. They would always argue about things, like Decadence versus Progress. Henry was for decadence, and Mel was for progress. Or they would fight about the South versus the North, which was the same thing.

We sat in Henry's garden, its bloom of a sweet unchanging profusion, but wild and overgrown. No one ever made the least attempt to do anything to it, such as cut the grass or do gardening. The only person who felt that a step should be taken in that direction was Mel, who dared to plant a little vegetable patch under the balcony. Henry protested wrathfully to this, and tried to make scathing comments, with disgust.

"I'm scared to go out in my garden because there's probably a little group of New England farmers having a harvest festival," Henry told Mel.

Mel came striding into the garden and said heatedly to us, "Where's Henry? I have something to say to him. I have a bone to pick with him."

"He's mad. He went off by himself," we said.

When Henry came back and saw Mel, he immediately brought up the vegetable patch.

"My garden was so dilapidated," Henry said, "before he ruined it"—pointing coldly to Mel.

"I dare you to taste my lettuce, Henry," said Mel. "Just taste it. Just let me fix you a salad from my crops."

"I refuse to taste your lettuce," said Henry. "And I can't believe a farmer has crops in my garden. My garden wasn't meant for crops. It was meant to be a garden. Garden. Can't you understand that? GODDAMNIT, CAN'T YOU UNDERSTAND THAT, GODDAMNIT?"

—⟫▪⟪—

"Can you lend me twenty dollars for a date?" said Mel.

"What do you mean, can I lend you twenty dollars for a date?" said Henry.

"I have a date with that girl upstairs. You're the one who introduced me to her."

"Why don't you go to dental school?" Henry said. "There's nothing wrong with having a trade. Why don't you go to trade school?"

Mel was an artist. Henry had a special loathing for artists, unless they were himself.

He continued to rave about dental school and pick fights.

We just sat in the garden until about two in the morning.

The next day I slept until three in the afternoon—it was Sunday— when Claude and Henry both came to my house and roused me from what was a stupor. It was one of those mornings where your first impulse is to cry. They took me to the park, which was a study in black and green—black people and green trees. It was like some tropic port. My bones felt dazed and weak. I made them bring me home. Then I just sat in my room and deteriorated.

Claude was leaving for New York.

—⟫▪⟪—

The afternoon before he left, we met in the park. He came walking along in his wrinkled khaki suit against all the green of the place, a rare sight. He came dawdling through the park. He meandered along, abstracted against the green, holding a stick, and appearing to be talking to a dog nearby. There was his fineness and the high bearing he had. We went by the old bandstand, the green-and-white striped awning.

Then I found him looking at me with an expression of sheer kindness in his eyes, just watching my face. I had seen this expression at certain times. It filled me with amazement. A shade of pure kindness came over his face, completely mild. It was the highest compliment he could have paid me, the gallant mildness in his calm scrutiny. He stood quietly, as though he just watched my face to see what I was really like. He could be so reserved, but did things straight from the heart.

"Louise, you have the truth in your eyes," he commented.

I did not know what he meant, but my heart still broke into a million pieces on the floor.

"If you would live more by your brains—it would be fruitful, Louise."

He just stood there mildly.

There was a certain grace he had, a physical thing, I admit, but an inexpressibly pretty thing. It was not really so physical, though. It was the symmetry that you find in people sometimes, a harmony which is very calming.

"It's never a hard responsibility to have only yourself to take care of," he said. "You should take care of someone else. It's not enough responsibility to just take care of yourself. But you know," he said, "I haven't noticed you taking such great care of yourself the past couple of years."

"I haven't noticed you taking such great care of yourself, either," I said. "But you take care of a lot of people," I said to him.

"I was going to start taking care of Saint," he said. "He was going to be my responsibility. I was going to manage everything. My father and I had been talking about it. He always thought he was too old to raise him."

We had a perplexed parting. He was going away. And so should I change the subject then? Already to New York?

"Why are you taking the train up there?" I said. "Why don't you fly?"

"Flying's for the birds," he said. "Get it?"

He started trying to make jokes. Lame-brained jokes. That was his personality. Actually, it did make me feel a little better.

Then we went to the bamboo grove.

-->⋈<--

The air seemed bitter around us when we parted. It was ambiguous. "You know how I feel," I said when he left. It was all I could muster.

He tried to be composed and reserved.

"I'll see you soon. I'll talk to you soon," Claude said.

There was an increasing melancholy in the air, my regret at leaving the sight of him.

-->⋈<--

He took the train from New Orleans to New York. Mr. Collier and Claude were both in tears at the station. They both had on sunglasses to hide it. This was the most maudlin occurrence I had ever seen involving them. Claude was glad he took the train so he would have a long time alone where no one he knew would be around. He was a haunted man on that train, his suit ineffably wrinkled, sunglasses on, either crying, in a daze, or ordering drinks at the bar.

The train leaves New Orleans and goes across Lake Pontchartrain, with rickety houses on stilts on the glittering lake. It then stops in Hattiesburg. It goes through the green South, until after Alexandria, it comes into the dying industrial North and up to the hub of the universe along the East Coast.

The first night Claude was in the dying industrial North he stayed at a Holiday Inn in a suburb of New Jersey. When he walked into the lobby, there was a band which started playing "The Impossible Dream." They were four men in electric-orange leisure suits with white patent leather shoes and then a banner came down out of the ceiling that said GUEST OF THE YEAR—WE WELCOME OUR 1,000,000TH GUEST OF THE YEAR!!!!

The manager and a group of Holiday Inn dignitaries rushed over and put garlands on Claude. The band started playing "I Gotta Be Me" and then "I Did It My Way."

Claude could not be alone the whole time because there was this huge celebration. Wherever he tried to go, in the restaurant or the lobby, the four men in leisure suits kept coming with him and surrounding him and playing "Feelings" or "People" or "I Gotta Be Me."

This thing could only have happened to Claude Collier.

It would have been different if he had been in his ordinary spirits. Then he probably would have liked it. But he was wearing the same wrinkled suit and sunglasses to hide his grief while men in leisure suits tormented him. Finally, though, Claude surrendered to it all. Since he was always surrounded by four men in orange leisure suits with instruments, finally he asked them if they could play "Smoke Gets in Your Eyes," and they did, and then he started screaming along with it and of course, in the end, made lifelong friends of them and of the manager and of the Holiday Inn dignitaries and of the waitresses with Dutch headpieces in the restaurant with the Norwegian theme.

They stocked his icebox with horns-of-plenty, and hung banners in his room. The telephone constantly rang.

"Can we do anything for you, sir?"

He told me about it all on the telephone, in a strangled voice. He brooded on the incident. He said it was symbolic.

--✦--

Then he took his irresolute American travels. He ran out of gas on interstate highways, flagging people down to take him to the service station, becoming great friends with them, forming lifelong bonds with them, their daughters falling in love with him, etc., while listening to disco music and rap singing on the radio or music videos on cable TVs in tawdry motels.

It was modern times up there. Claude would take out binoculars on the side of the Northern highway and make enthusiastic notes about the terrain. He carried a pad with the legend Things I Gotta

Do Today, and even when he had nothing to do, which was always, he was constantly making notes of things, I don't know exactly what, and his pockets were bulging with lists and notes at the end of the day. At tawdry motels they littered the bureau, small crumpled papers and scraps with indecipherable notes on them.

Ideas. He said they were ideas. He said they were ideas and that they had a future before them. He would pace briskly around hotel rooms or tawdry motel rooms working on his ideas and chewing pencils and eating erasers. Then he would go out and take brisk walks and look through his binoculars at fallen industrial-waste sites and ruined Northern factories.

He took pictures, he took notes. He was always full of cheerful, enthusiastic habits.

◆◆◆

Driving along in his rented car, which had a weird tape-recorded computerized message that blared from the rafters whenever he opened the door, "A *door is ajar*," he would almost get in wrecks when it came on or crane his head around to look at girls, almost getting in wrecks.

His effect on women was that total strangers in restaurants or hotel lobbies would come up to him and say, "Excuse me, but are you all right? You look a little pale. Is something wrong? Can I get you a glass of water?"

He would probably find Yankee girls, I thought. He would probably find Yankee girls, and they would be impressed by his Southern-boy crackpot streak, and he wouldn't be as obvious as the young men they knew, and the young men they knew would be artists and writers and intellectuals and then they would see Claude, sitting there, waiting for them somewhere, wearing a suit, being polite, and with the kindness in his face. They would be Boston girls, descendants of famous Yankees, healthy and sober, standing on black-and-white checkered floors in North Shore mansions, going to commencement parties, graduating from college, and Claude Collier would take them out on binges until four in the morning.

I could see it all.

Then he drove on, up through the blue aisles of Maine, the green aisles of trees in Vermont, to Trois-Rivieres, Sainte Foy, and Quebec. The air was so sweet and blue, a climate unknown in the Gulf South. Everyone looked so healthy—it was no wonder, with their climate. They were in visible contrast to Claude, with his pale dissipated face—no matter how elegant—looking stark, his Southern-boy crackpot streak. It was very different from what he knew, so sterling and upright, unlike the steamy gardens of New Orleans.

⋯⟩𝔼❰⋯

He spent the nights in motels, tawdry motels, and watched late movies on TV, and dreamed of his city—vegetables rotting in the French Market, polite aged black men with cigars, the tepid waters of the Gulf Coast—gentleness, dilapidation, and refuge. Driving along the Gulf Coast at Biloxi, with its ruined grandeur, its air of neglect, its segregated beaches (Danse de Negres), the languishing Rigolets—whenever I go to the Gulf Coast, I think of the Civil War, and that we lost it is always plain. Something noble in the Northern air affected Claude, but he had that conflict between North and South, an attraction which the one has for the other, yet from an adversary standpoint—a certain form of love. But Claude had the profound chastisement of the defeated party, which the victorious one can never know.

⋯⟩𝔼❰⋯

The humidity in New Orleans is unhealthy and lethargic, even if the gray days are so gentle down the Avenue, underneath the arch of oaks. In the East—with ivy and a cool spring, rectitude and high ideals, severity, victory—it belongs to the cold weather, to the change of seasons, not to the Latin nights. The Latin nights are more cynical, jaded, and frivolous. There is in them no earnestness, such as there is in the North. But loyalty and gratitude ate at Claude's heart for what was his. It is possible to become daunted—as he could have been called those nights when he sat in motel rooms making lists of all the addresses he had ever had, all the apartments he had ever lived in, all the telephone numbers, all the highways he had driven on, and then the names of everyone that he had ever known. He went back to Boston, rolling through potholes and reconciled to solitude, for once in his life, having gin and tonics in a café before it got dark by the old City Hall, by the graveyards that always seemed rainy in their one square of green.

In June, Mr. Collier and I made a visit. I sat on the banks of the Charles River with Claude on deck chairs in the night, the ones I kept folded up in my car to remind me, two deck chairs in the Northern night with Claude. He was talking about how normal it was up there. It was just something so normal, he said.

It is true, New Orleans was never normal. Being normal was one quality New Orleans just never had.

Then he who never talked about himself, who had no introspection, did venture this one opinion.

"I'm such a normal person. I'm just a normal guy. I can't believe I'm not a country lawyer or something like that. I can't believe that someone as normal as I am could have had so much trouble being normal."

Then he looked calmly across the river to the lights in Boston, sitting in his deck chair.

It was commencement time, with green-and-white striped tents set up in all the gardens by the Harvard houses, and the men wearing top hats and tails, gray silk and black pinstripe. Mr. Collier went to his class reunion.

Mr. Collier carried a black umbrella open against the sun—a Louisiana custom, umbrellas for the shade. But people stared at him at commencement, as he walked around in his seersucker suit, his tall figure conspicuous in the crowd, his large black umbrella open over his head on that clear crisp day, in that sterner stuff the North is made of.

We were walking around and saw a poem engraved into the pavement.

"What is this quote, Louise?" said Mr. Collier.

I said it was from Henry Wadsworth Longfellow, although I was practically too hung over to read the lines, from a party Claude and I went to the night before.

Mr. Collier looked at me, ecstatic. That was the thing that made him happy, whether you could identify a certain excerpt, or if you could speak in ancient Greek. Not to mention if you could cite unexpected key changes in a score. What a refuge that fellow had against the world.

"You are the artistic one, Louise," he said. "Persevere; it suits you."

⟶⟡⟵

Things can sometimes be too poignant. Sometimes there is far too much poignance in things. It was like that in Cambridge—too many green-and-white striped tents with parties, too much gaiety and promise and good weather.

It could not have been more different from Latin American Night in the Quarter, some months before.

⟶⟡⟵

I was sitting in Claude's room later. We were sitting in his room, which was, as yet, unfurnished because he didn't know if he was going to stay in Boston, although he had taken a room, and there was something curiously sordid about it. We were eating pathetic wilted cheese sandwiches. The lettuce was wilted and it was so pathetic somehow, my profound love for him, sitting with him being so alone and pathetic. That's what I thought love was, being in the most pathetic part of someone's solitude.

"My life is in Total Chaos," he said.

I looked at his old plaid bathrobe and pale ankles and pathetic bedroom slippers and the same wave swept over me again and I knew he was the only person I had ever loved—and very possibly would ever love.

"Sweetie," he said, "could you go get me a carton of Marlboros?"

"But the doctor said you're not supposed to smoke."

"I know but, sweetheart, could you do that for me, and Louise, could you bring me some hot tamales, too?"

Mr. Collier sat with his head in his hands, closeted in his office. A tape recorder emitted clipped, garbled sounds: the recitation of Homer in the ancient Greek. It was one of the days on which Mr. Collier went to his young son's grave.

I was home for the summer, our trip to Boston long since faded from the world. I was experiencing life in the slow lane—the South.

Mr. Collier was spending a lot of his time with a Jesuit priest named Father Boudreaux, who was tutoring him in ancient Greek. Originally there were several other people in the tutorial, but it had dwindled down to just Mr. Collier and Father Boudreaux, who had become inseparable, and who referred to themselves as the Opsimathic Society. You would see them strolling down the Avenue against the raging sky, Father Boudreaux's black habit billowing behind him in the breeze, Mr. Collier with his cigar.

He was dignified and wry.

"My wife and I are going to the cemetery this afternoon to see my son's grave," he said.

Then he cut a stern swath out of the room.

That summer the only comforts were (1) air-conditioning and (2) rainy weather.

Then the summer pursued to the fall, and to the winter, etc.

Claude had been gone for four months. All I did was go to disco bars with the clerks at the office. I wished I could get the decency to lead a regular life: to be a struggling teacher or a struggling newlywed, or to nurse soldiers on war-torn battlefields—or to give up my Wastrel Youth.

I went to the Customs House on Canal Street to deliver a maritime brief and saw old gentlemen with mustaches who had worked there for fifty years, quietly fixing the foreign trade. I wished that I could be more like them. "Rectitude is a virtue celebrated not by cries of joy, but by serenity, fixed or habitual."

I went jogging through the park in the afternoon. I was not athletic, but Mr. Collier always said, "Take exercise, be moderate, and lead a regulated life. You should lead a regulated life."

The park was like France, like an afternoon on a boulevard with strollers and promenaders in the elegance of the oaks, whose branches made a roof of leaves.

⟶⟩⊞⟨⟵

Oh, I forgot to tell about Percy Chumbley.

Percy Chumbley was one of my suitors. Percy Chumbley was the most revolting thing known to man.

That's all I have to say about him.

⟶⟩⊞⟨⟵

One night I got a phone call from Mel, Henry Laines' former neighbor, the Northerner from Vermont. He was about to return to his homeland, he said.

The whole time he was in New Orleans he acted as if he were a tragic exile in outer Siberia.

Yankees are often that way. Millions of Southerners go up North to live and see the world, but how many Yankees do you catch moving down to Alabama, say? Therefore, we Southerners can understand the North because we have seen it, we lived there. But you Yankees would never just move to Alabama for two years. As a result, Southerners are actually the less provincial, contrary to popular thought.

But of course change is severely distressing no matter what it is, and either party is like a fish out of water when not where he belongs, like Homer, mournfully longing for his native land, his distant city, wondering if he will see it again.

It's a trap in the mind.

⟶⟩⊞⟨⟵

Claude called frequently, but from funny-seeming parties with people screaming in the background and 1920s fox-trot music, remote and scratchy flapper violins.

I did not know quite what to make of it.

What was he doing? On the telephone, I told him Mel called to say good-bye and sent regards.

"He called, you say?"

"Just called."

"Just called to say good-bye? Just telephoned? Hello and good-bye, so to speak?"

"That's right," I said.

"Well, what did he say?" Claude asked.

"He said he just wanted to get in touch with you when he went back up East."

"Then what did you say?"

"I gave him the address."

"Then what did he say?"

"He thanked me, Claude."

"Then what did you say?"

"I said you're welcome."

"He probably loves you," Claude said. "You probably make him go mad with desire. What about that? You make men go mad with desire."

"Oh, God."

"Oh, God? Who's over there? Are you alone? What are you doing? Where have you been? Who were you with? What did you have for dinner last night? What did you have for breakfast today? Did you have scrambled eggs?"

I could hear people screaming in the background as though at funny-seeming parties.

We were disconnected.

Then he called back.

"What happened?" I said.

"Oh, I knocked over a table."

There were people screaming in the background, and music.

"What is it like up there?" I said. "What is going on? How is it?"

"Up and down."

"In and out, so to speak?"

Then we were disconnected again.

Minutes later the phone rang.

"What happened this time?"

"Oh, I knocked that same table over again," Claude said. "Wait—

this phone is coming out of the socket." Then there were screams of laughter in the background, crashes, and music, and we were disconnected again.

--><::--

I pictured him with Yankee girls. He would probably go to their rooms and ask them small, infuriating questions. They would be standing in kitchens frying eggs, and he would probably stand there in wonderment saying, "You're frying eggs? Scrambled eggs? What time is it? Why are you cooking them right now at this particular hour? What does it all mean?" Then he would send them weird clippings in the mail, pick them up in his car with Louisiana license plates (The Bayou State). How could it help but wring their hearts?

I could picture everything that would probably happen. I could see it all. The doorbell would ring, and some Yankee girl would go to answer it. There would stand Claude, in a seersucker suit, and her heart would immediately break into a million pieces on the floor. At the end of the night, he would be screaming the lyrics to "Smoke Gets in Your Eyes" and then possibly he would pass out in the bathtub, fully clothed. Then he would try to get up and crack his head against the porcelain, and she would have to take him to the emergency room to get stitches, and all the nurses would love him and he would ask them out on dates.

But I knew the Yankee girls would love him, his mild normal handsomeness. He was always calm—except at the latest hour of the night—but at other times he always had a calm logic in his demeanor, polite and attentive.

Yankee girls probably usually sat around having philosophically inquiring conversations about the meaning of art. But Claude would never talk about serious things. He was always too busy making lame-brained jokes or talking about the small things. He would probably tell them that the dress they were wearing reminded him of some huge thing—all he wanted to do was plummet to the depths of factuality about what you were doing at that exact moment, and what you were really like. He was just a simple dark-haired Tareyton smoker, completely wry.

My heart was not trained to love anyone but him. I could only love one person. This was my innate principle. It would disrupt the nervous system to be otherwise. It goes against nature to be otherwise. I cannot just transfer my affections, for they are carved in stone, and were decreed three billion years before this ocean rolled.

--❯❚❮--

It was the last day of the World Series. All the clerks in the office were men obsessed. They all changed into nuts and rolled TV sets into the reception rooms, and put on silly sports caps. It was also the night of a famous boxing match in the Superdome, which generated the same screwball enthusiasm. Then, too, it was the day the furniture was being changed, and movers came into my office at nine o'clock. They brought in one desk and removed its predecessor, which, all together, took about seven minutes, and then they said that it was time for their break.

"Okay then," they drawled, heaving sighs of exertion as after a long, hard job done well, "we on our break now."

"Wait," I said. "Pardon?"

"Time for our break."

"Time for your break? Time for your break? But you just brought in one desk," I said.

"We on our break now, though."

"But you just got here. You came in at nine, and now it's ten minutes later."

They were large, robust, handsome black men making jokes. Then they all lit up cigarettes and were hanging around in the reception room with the clerks. I was dejected. Earl Battaglio, the born-again Christian, came in to my office and told me to cheer up.

"Look to the sky, Louise," he said.

"What?"

"Just look to the sky," he said.

"What do you mean, look to the sky?"

"For your personal relationship with the Lord," he allowed.

It was Friday and the secretaries were in a good mood because they had before them an unlimited amount of time within a three-day period to drink and go to disco bars. I spent most of the day calling fancy restaurants and making reservations for the lawyers and visiting dignitaries, like the Russians. They had a lot of cocktail parties at the office. It was often said that law school was the hardest time you would ever spend in the law. After that, it became a party. The lawyers in my office were dignified society men and they were very scholarly, but it did seem like they spent a good deal of time playing tennis, hunting ducks, or, like Mr. Collier, listening to ancient Greek or opera, which, of course, was his idea of a party.

⋆⁓⊃⧫⊂⁓⋆

I was getting kind of drunk from the Friday afternoon cocktail party which was going on in the reception room. The clerks were standing around wearing Madras sports jackets and bright green or yellow golfing slacks. The office had dark red Oriental rugs, dark red curtains, chandeliers, and dark rosewood furniture. I was surrounded by fine old men in conservative suits and silk vests. Except Mr. LaSalle—who always wore those cheap black-and-white checkered sports jackets, like men who go to the racetrack every day, and garish avocado-colored shirts. But he warmed my heart—a seriously silly person, on the whole.

He was telling me one of his stories about the famous. "I remember one time," he said, "I was with my sister. We were real small. This was about a million years ago. Ancient history, you know? We were walking down in the Quarter—we used to live down there—and Edgar Allan Poe was lying in the gutter outside of Galatoire's. Edgar Allan Poe, dawlin. Sure, dawlin. I'm not lying. I'm dying if I'm lying."

"You and your sister, I swear," I said.

Then he started talking about his War Experiences. His War Experiences involved being sent off at the train station in New Orleans, surrounded by weeping relatives, getting off at Biloxi, where he was met by a band of cousins, and attending dinner dances under the tent on the Gulf at the Palmetto Inn.

"Dawlin, when I think of Biloxi, I could cry. When I think about Biloxi, I get tears in my eyes. Aw, yeah," he said in a tone which implied that his listeners were in a Stupor of Incredulity.

-->≈<--

At five o'clock I crossed Canal Street into the Quarter with some of the clerks to have a drink at the Royal Orleans. It was one of those mob scenes that we get in this town at frequent intervals year-round. We rely on the tourist dollar. Jammed in the narrow streets were black Cadillacs and Texans and people with cameras. I wonder in my heart, since the place is so beautiful, what it would actually be like if the Quarter were as still and deserted and lethargic as all the rest of town.

We sat in the Royal Orleans at the ground floor bar, viewing the scene through French windows. Then we went to a side street to an oyster bar. The bar had yellow pin-striped wallpaper and a dark mahogany bureau with *The New York Times* in stacks selling for a fortune each. We walked to another bar, with chairs set out on the sidewalk by large shuttered doors, the white marble Fifth Circuit Court of Appeals across the street, with magnolia trees and the calm bustle of a side street late at night in the balmy air.

I had taken to walking all around the Quarter until its air of debauch wearied me—I even walked down Bourbon, that height of ruin, Friday evening after work, past the strippers, the ruined architecture, and thought of my memories. It is not the frailty of my memories, but the strength of them, that causes me to recollect. Certain figures passing down the street, of life in a small town, contain a sense of fate, for each has his noble secret and each his handsome drama.

The weather had turned fine. Dark fell. I looked into the glittering night. Suddenly, a parade came out of nowhere and passed through the unsuspecting street, heralded by African drumbeats in the distance vaguely, then the approach of jazz, the smell of sweet olive, ambrosia, the sense of impending spectacle. Then it passed in its fleeting beauty, this glittering dirge, and, as suddenly as it came, I was left, rather stunned, in its wake.

It is this passing parade which I chronicle.

-->≈<--

Transfixed by the huge palm trees on Rampart Street, silhouetted in the tropic night, I pursued back to the Lafayette Hotel, to pay my debt to society.

The Lafayette Hotel was a place whose moment of glory had long since faded from the world. Its moment of glory was definitely past. Passed forever from the world. It had an extremely seedy air. The decor was red plush and cobweb, with grandiose marble domes and fixtures. The floor was in white tile. Cracked leather armchairs stood empty next to dying potted palms. A grandiose staircase dominated the lobby, which held only the barest traces of the former glory of the Lafayette Hotel. There were portraits of General Lee at the Surrender. The lobby was deserted, except for one bloodshot person in a trench coat, who sat clutching a paper bag. A languid jazz band could be heard from the courtyard beyond, which was the bar.

There was a crescent moon in a starless sky. The bar was packed with people lined up against it standing up, under the ceiling fan, in the sweltering night, with the tables and chairs in the courtyard.

I ran into Mr. LaSalle.

"Hey, dawlin, how'd you get to be so cute?" he said. "Where'd you get those brown eyes?"

Henry Laines came up.

"May I join you?" he asked with elaborate politeness.

"Sure, dawlin," said Mr. LaSalle

Then Mr. LaSalle started philosophizing to me about women. "You see, dawlin, women like to be led. Women are the weaker sex. It's human nature, precious," he said.

"Cut it out, you two," said Henry. As a rule, Southerners do not like philosophical conversations.

"I saw a friend of yours the other night!" said a fellow named George Sweeney loudly, coming up to me. "Claude Collier," he said.

"Claude Collier?" I said weakly.

"Isn't he your boyfriend?" said George Sweeney. "I ran into him in New York when I was there." George Sweeney smiled lewdly. He was a very corrupt person, and he had this strange dashing corruption that most women seemed to like. "Well, that boy is just one of the greatest athletes ever to come out of Louisiana," said George Sweeney.

What a preposterous thing to say, I thought.

"How have you been, Louise?"

"Well, I've been on some crying jags lately."

"Touch of the poet," he said scornfully into his Jack Daniel's. "Louise, you're still the prettiest girl in town." Some of his stupid Memphis sweet talk. "Don't wait around for your boyfriend."

--◆◆◆--

"Did you hear about Mr. Walker?" I said.

"No, tell me," said the receptionist.

"He's having a Nervous Breakdown," I reported.

One of the lawyers walked by and started coughing loudly and looking in my direction significantly. He walked into an outer reception room and stood in the doorway, calling out, "Louise, could you step in here for a minute, please?"

This lawyer was about thirty-five years old, and he was from Macon, Georgia, and had a strong drawl, blond hair, and always wore large black sunglasses that looked like 1950. His name was Mr. Milburn. I watched through the doorway as he went ahead of me to some chairs in the corner of the room. He had a rather smoldering sexuality, I would say. He wore a gray suit with a silk vest and had taken off his coat, and had a cumbersome stride — one of his legs dragged as though it were paralyzed down from the knee — and he always reminded me of an eighth-rate movie about a sultry antebellum plantation with torture and lust in which the young landowner had the same dragging foot, lunging down grandiose stairways, wearing sweat-soaked white lace shirts open to the waist and high black riding boots, carrying a whip, having sex with mulattoes, and then dropping them in huge vats of boiling water.

When I entered the room, he looked up and said, "Hi, young lady. I heard you talking to Annie about Mr. Walker, young lady. That can be personal slander. Young lady, you shouldn't be spreading rumors. Now, I know you have more discretion than that. Am I right, young lady?"

"Yes, sir—you are right," I said.

Then he started getting bored with my company and picked up a *Wall Street Journal*. I went back to Annie's desk, unnoticed.

"Okay, Louise," she said in her gravel voice. "What about Mr. Walker?"

"He's having a Nervous Breakdown," I said.

My morals were deteriorating.

"Big deal. I'm having one too," said Annie, lighting a cigarette.

❖

The clubfoot lawyer from Macon, Georgia, was also the author of *Texas Business Law*. The author of *Texas Business Law* also wrote *Texas Governors*, *Texas Wildflowers*, and *You Can Be Special Because You Are*, all of which I had to proofread, taking huge amounts of time out of my life.

Of course, I didn't really mind. It added new weirdos to my life. But then he wrote a novel, which he asked me to read. I thought it was Unnecessarily Lurid.

Then he wrote another novel, which he asked me to read, and I thought it also was Unnecessarily Lurid. I told him I didn't think life was really like that. At least I didn't think the lawyer's life was like that. At least I hope the lawyer's life was not like that.

The novels had rape, murder, and decapitation. I doubt whether people in their real lives go around getting decapitated all the time. But in his novels people got decapitated all the time, and would have torture and lust on plantations.

❖

The next day I was late. The author of *Texas Business Law*, who probably wanted to decapitate me, was sitting at my desk, something sinister about him, yet something harmless and soft-spoken.

"Young lady, you're late," he said. "You can't just walk in late. This is the real world."

But he had a broad, helpless smile across his face, like an indulgent father.

❖

They were having a cocktail party for the staff. Mr. LaSalle brought his wife. He called her Mama.

"Louise, this is Mama."

She, in turn, called him Junior.

Mr. LaSalle, holding a cocktail, had that limpid, deadpan hilarious look in his eyes. The lawyer with the dragging foot came up and said, "Did you get those registered letters in the mail this morning, young lady?"

He always called me young lady, as though it were my name.

"No, I threw them in the river," I said.

I don't know why.

Breakdowns.

I think I was having a Breakdown.

"I took it over to the park and threw it in the lagoon," I said.

I went back to my desk to clean up, except I accidentally lit the trash can on fire.

I was madly trying to put it out and he was saying, "What is going on in here?"

"Fire!" I said.

The next day they told me they thought I should take a vacation. Then that lawyer called me into his office. He was sitting at his desk. His old-fashioned 1950s black sunglasses lay on the desk.

"Hi, young lady," he said.

"Hi."

"Young woman, do you know Earl Battaglio?" he then said.

"Yes, I do," I said.

Then the lawyer lapsed into a beatific silence. He looked to the ceiling. "You know, my wife Betty put on a few pounds when we were married. Once I asked her why. And do you know what she said? She said, 'Well, Calhoun, when I married you I guess I just got so plumb satisfied, that I turned to fat.'"

I smiled nervously. "How interesting," I said.

Then he told me that they wanted me to go up to Richmond to file the papers in a shoplifting case which I had typed the depositions for, so I could get away for a while.

This was a case we had about a society man accused of shoplifting a watch from a jewelry store in Richmond, Virginia. The man was either crazy or in trouble, because he was in high finance and high society and there was no reason why he should shoplift. The jury had convicted him, but the case was being appealed, and the papers had to be filed in Richmond.

I took the train.

~>⊠<~

The train station in Richmond was filled with pathetically deferential doddering old black men and other species of complete wrecks. Everyone in the station was a wreck. Everyone had a heavy Southern accent. The whole atmosphere was sultry and defeated. At the platform, where a huge crowd of beleaguered Southern wrecks had assembled, suddenly a parade of about twenty-five jolly Southern black men in white butler's coats descended onto the train before us. It was downright macabre. Finally, we boarded the train, and I have never seen a train like that before. It was the Panama Express—because when it came back down, it went to Florida, like macabre Southerners going to macabre Florida. Eighty-five percent of the passengers were black, and each car had its white-coated black butler.

There were old-fashioned dining cars and sleeping cars and smoking rooms. I got the name wrong—not the Panama Express but the West Palm Beach. The night was black and the countryside doomed and deserted. There was a huge confusion on the train due to its lateness (it had been late) and the crowds.

~>⊠<~

I went to breakfast at Chesterfield's in Richmond. Breakfast costs $1.25 there, and the waitresses say, "Girl, what you want?"

I stayed at the Jefferson Hotel. It was completely deserted. Then suddenly, at about eight o'clock that night, a wedding party from Lexington traipsed in for a reception. Curiously, they all looked as though they had just stepped out of the French Riviera or Monte Carlo from jet-set casinos. The young men had tuxedos and white tie and tails and long hair, or else punk-rock outfits; and the girls had high-fashion dresses in weird avant-garde styles. I regarded them for a while, enraptured by their glamour, and then went up to bed.

❖

The next day, coming home, it was not until Mobile, Alabama, that I recognized the Gulf South again, with wide oak-lined avenues and mansions, dark green shade, iron grillework, palm trees, and shotgun houses. There were parks, dark greenness bounded by black wrought iron. The Gulf breeze was mild.

When I delivered the papers to the born-again, clubfoot lawyer from Macon, Georgia, it turned out that I had forgotten to get the signature of the clerk of court at Richmond.

It was then that he fired me.

It was pouring down rain, with crashes of thunder and an electrical storm. Every once in a while there would be a huge crack of thunder. I was facing the window, and I could see the river and the central business district.

"I have some bad news for you, young lady," he said.

I knew I had some proofreading errors in his books.

"Is it *Texas Business Law?*" I said.

"Worse."

"*Texas Governors?*"

"Worse."

"*You Can Be Special Because You Are?*"

There was an ominous silence.

"I'm fired."

"That's right."

❖

Vanity is worse than any vice, but the line between vanity and self-respect is somehow very thin.

I walked out, composed, and looked at my office for the last time, with the portrait above my desk that I always used to stare at, of Lincoln delivering the Gettysburg Address on a battlefield. I thought for the last time of the lawyer from Macon, Georgia, trudging up the stairs with his dragging foot, wearing a gold lamé short-sleeved shirt that he would always wear on Saturday, with his black 1950s sunglasses.

It was gray and black out—gray sky, black people.

Everything was mild.

I walked into a movie theater on Canal Street, and everything seemed so mild, like France, at four o'clock on a normal day. The movie theater was one of those ancient ornate ones with red plush velvet everywhere. The ticket takers were lying around on the stairs looking out at the street with the sallow faces of saints, black men wearing gold theater uniforms, sprawled on the stairs looking out to Canal Street as though it were some slow jazz party.

Carnival, in fact, was pending. The floats were coming over from across the river from their den in Gretna, across the Mississippi River Bridge, tropical papier-mâché crafts with drumbeats in the distance vaguely.

Uptown, my relief increased.

I would devote myself to the pursuit of beauty. Indolence is necessary to wisdom. I would be a student of truth. My lamp would be lit, late into the night. I would smoke too many cigarettes late at night and get the elations of poetry, like at college.

⚜

The parades started.

There were bare bulbs lit up in the trees, white canvas grandstands, mobs of people under the oaks, police on horses, and the kings and dukes on horses with plumes sticking up out of their headpieces while they toasted the crowds, with their silk harlequin masks.

I could not believe my eyes when I turned around and saw the parade coming up the Avenue. This beauty was remarkable here. But there was also "this mad solitude." I did not understand it. I only understood of it that it was not right. Do people go straight from one person's arms to another? People conduct that way, perhaps that is how people conduct. They are lucky.

The Duke of Spain went back into the Garden District on Mardi Gras Day with his white satin cape flying in the breeze behind him, in an exquisite false spring, for the weather was sweet and in it there was the scent of gardenia. Some young men wearing black pin-striped suits and straw skimmer hats with black ribbons set far back on their heads strolled up the Avenue, near to marching bands of harlequins playing jazz up the Avenue and under the oaks, with wrought-iron lace and columned mansions in the Garden District and elderly social pinnacles in white tie and tails coming out of iron gates, bowing down paths. Such madcap elegance was never elsewhere seen. At the end is the heart-heaving beauty of Comus, that glittering dirge, bidding farewell to the flesh, with its last raptures. "What hath night to do with sleep? Night hath better sweets to prove."

There were such sights, the Zulu parade, in which I was promised a coconut by the Gospel Soul Children, and in the end Comus, that glittering dirge, at last in the night, inexpressibly gaudy and beautiful as it passes along, bidding farewell to the flesh. There are always drumbeats haunting the parade, and flambeaux and harlequins in satin and silk.

❖

I went to Grand Isle, at the bottom of Louisiana, at the very end of it out to sea, Land's End some call it, where people used to go, to old-fashioned hotels. The farther down toward Grand Isle I got, the more I could feel the passion in the land, the farther and farther I got toward the edge. It is not in Louisiana a stern magnificence, with pure noble cold sea air. We have a different magnificence—everyone in their harlequin masks, it is regular to them, in their satin and plumes. But at Grand Isle, at the very end of the land out to sea, there were the elements. I crossed over the bridge to the island, and the swamps were shimmering in the golden cold air, the marshes and swamps were glittering—and then I saw some fields of wheat.

I drove down Bayou Lafourche all morning to get there. The weather was cold and pure like the North. The farther down I got toward Grand Isle, alone and finding a passion in the land, the more I thought of the wasted years.

❖

I went to the Colliers' house.

Byron was sitting in his "car" in the driveway of the house.

"You married, Louise?" he said.

"Oh—no no," I said.

"Neither me."

This must have struck him as amusing, our mutual unmarried condition, for he chuckled.

"Where Mr. Claude stay at now?" said Byron.

"He stays in Boston."

"You should stay by your mama," said Byron. "My sister stay by my mama. My daddy got married to another lady. My mama, she booted him out the house. He could go to his other wives' house, that's what I said. But he said no. He say he left his shoes over by my mama's house and she won't let him in, so he say he's to take her to court. He tried to strangle my mama."

According to Byron, his father had five wives.

"My mama said I could take my shoes off," he commented, showing me his feet. He looked at me shyly. Then he said, "I asked my mama where that Saint stay at now. She said Jesus Mercy Lord real quiet. So I told my mama, I said I know where he stay—over on First Street—and she told me, because then she say, 'He dead, sugar.'"

I stared.

"Don't you go in the street with that car," I said, and then I walked into the house.

─→✠←─

Mrs. Collier was sitting at her desk paying bills. Mr. Collier was lying in his bed fully clothed in a tuxedo, his hands clasped behind his head, staring at the ceiling. It was seven o'clock in the evening. He was muttering to himself.

"What is he doing?" I asked Mrs. Collier.

"He's memorizing Dante's *Inferno*."

"I thought he was memorizing the *Odyssey*," I said.

"Also the *Odyssey*. Tonight he is meeting with Father Boudreaux at Antoine's. The Opsimathic Society, such as it is, meets there now once a week."

I walked back into the bedroom.

─→✠←─

" 'In the middle of the journey of our life, I came to myself within a dark wood where the straight way was lost,' " he quoted with melancholy.

Then he quoted something else. " 'Sweet life is almost over for me, my teeth are falling out, and my hair is white. Sweet life is almost over.' "

I went back to Mrs. Collier at her desk.

"Is he all right?" I asked. "He does not seem quite right."

"Louise, it's too much ancient Greek. I just don't know. Go talk to him."

"I have bade adieu to all species of affection," Mr. Collier said. "Books and music are the only things which testify to the nobility of the human soul. They alone assuage the intolerable tedium of society."

He had a queer gleam in his eye. He rose from his bed, in his tuxedo, and motioned me to follow as he went to the kitchen.

The table was covered with wine bottles.

"What are these wine bottles doing on this table?" he said. "I will tell you—books and music."

He fell silent.

"What do you mean, sir?" I said.

"Come this way."

He proceeded to the library. He took a piece of parchment from his desk.

"This is an actual decree from Photius to the Eastern patriarchs in the year 867. They let me take it out of the rare book room at Tulane. I require a complete copy of this letter in English—could you get it for me, Louise?"

He studied my face.

"Yes, of course," I said. "Certainly I can do it for you, sir. Anything you say. I can get it at Tulane."

"I'm studying Byzantine empires," Mr. Collier said.

"Quite right," I said.

"There's nothing quite like a Byzantine empire," said Mr. Collier.

"I imagine that's quite true," I said.

After that, I began to visit him every day; I made it a rule. I had no job to go to myself, and he didn't go to his job anymore, either. We had all the time in the world. He kept taking up new interests. He acquired an interest in lives of the saints. Religion was not among his comforts, however. His interest in lives of the saints was not religious.

—)BK(—

"Man longs to live but is forced to die, and how can any man be said to live as he longs to live who does not even live as long as he longs to live. Of course, if he should long to die, then he does not even long to live, let alone to live as he longs to live. If a man is living as he longs to live—"

"Louis, please," said Mrs. Collier, "stop it."

"But it's St. Augustine, Jane."

"It's unhealthy!" said Mrs. Collier.

"Just listen to one more thing. I have one more thing to say. I was leafing through my *Lives of the Saints* the other day, and came upon a curious passage about St. Augustine. It seems he was walking along the beach one day thinking about his discourse on the Trinity, when all of a sudden he saw a little boy. St. Augustine asked the little boy what he was doing, and the boy said he was filling up a hole in the sand with water, and he intended to pour all the waters of the entire sea into the little hole he had made. 'That is impossible,' said St. Augustine. The little boy replied, 'Not more impossible than for a finite mind to contain the infinite.'— Then the little boy vanished into thin air," Mr. Collier concluded.

—)BK(—

"In a certain way, Jane, that puts a new light on the hypostatic union."

"What's the hypostatic union?"

"Ah, the hypostatic union," he trailed off, fondly.

—)BK(—

Shortly after that, to Mrs. Collier's grief, Mr. Collier went to see a mystic. The mystic told him that the soul of a child was often reborn into the same family. That's when Mr. Collier started looking at me strangely.

"When are you planning to go up and visit Claude?" he said.

"I'm not exactly sure," I said.

"Have you two discussed marriage?" he said.

Mrs. Collier gasped.

"Once we discussed marriage," I said. "He tripped. Then he fell down."

"Not a good sign," said Mr. Collier.

"Louis, what are you saying?" said Mrs. Collier.

"I apologize," Mr. Collier said. "I hope I haven't overstepped the bounds of decency and decorum." Then he went back to his book, *The Universe As I See It*, by Albert Einstein.

⁓⟫▦⟪⁓

Mr. Collier said to his wife, "Jane, we must go to Persia. We must look firsthand at Byzantine artifacts."

"I am not going to Persia, Louis. Persia is not the answer."

"But, Jane—Byzantine empires!"

"Byzantine empires are not the answer for me. I watch cable TV and music videos. I'm not involved in the ancient world. I'm involved in the present. Why must you study ancient times?"

"To improve the mind," Mr. Collier said, quoting another great man.

⁓⟫▦⟪⁓

Byron was sitting, as usual, in front of the Colliers' house.

"You seen Mr. Claude?" he asked me.

"Not yet."

"Neither he or his brother at home."

"Byron, why don't you come by my house tomorrow? We could play. I know some card games."

"You going in to see Mr. Collar?" he said. "He act kind of strange, that's what my mama said."

"Well, yes," I said, "I'm going in. Want to come?"

"No, because I'm the guard. I guard the house."

"Well, that's very nice," I said.

"My mama say she wished she never took her marriage vowels," Byron observed.

"Vows. Marriage vows."

"That's because my daddy has five wives."

"Listen, you precious, I'm going inside. Be careful you don't go in the street with that car."

—◆—

Mr. Collier asked me to go to the grave. I mean, he asked me to visit the grave for him.

So I went to the grave. A workman came up to me and said, "Is that fellow your father, who comes out here all the time?"

"All the time? All the time?"

"Like every day."

"No, he's a friend of mine."

"It's a funny thing. He comes out here every day. He gives me money. On All Saints' Day he gave me a fifty-dollar bill. He slips it into my coat pocket, never mentions it—it's a tip. He's supporting me."

I didn't say anything.

"He's a fine old fellow, isn't he?" said the man.

Then I saw a society man walking toward me wearing an olive drab suit and a bow tie. He carried a black umbrella to shade himself against the heat of the morning, the whitewashed vaults without trees.

"Excuse me," he said, "I see you're visiting Saint Collier's grave."

"Yes," I said.

"You're a friend of Claude's?"

"Yes, I am, a friend of the family," I said.

"I've known Louis Collier since . . . well, long before you were around."

"You have?"

"He's a great character. I can never tell when he's kidding, after all these years."

"I know."

"He once did something for me," began the man. "—Oh, he's done a lot of things for me . . . " the man trailed off. "He is one of a kind."

"I know what you mean."

"He's not looking well," said the man. "It could be he's spending too much time out here. He looks pale to me. Does he look pale to you?"

I regarded the graveyard society I had just met. The workman was standing a few feet away, smoking a cigar—probably a donation from Mr. Collier. The society man closed his umbrella. He sighed. The workman leaned on his rake.

→⊰⊱←

Mr. Collier was sitting in his library in his chair. Ordinarily a handsome man, his features derived further character even from a pallor and dark circles under the eyes, which gave an air of grace and weariness to Mr. Collier.

"I've never been so attached to someone," he said, "as I was to my little boy. But he is gone, he is gone."

There was something incomprehensible about it. It was beyond his grasp, he felt. It was beyond his grasp to know exactly why it had such intensity now.

Some men can be loyal only to ideals, which they cling to with the greatest tenacity. With a great ideal to be loyal to, their loyalty would be immense. They are too gentle, at last, to cherish something actual, something concrete.

A year after he got married, Mr. Collier received what he took to be an injury from his wife. An episode not uncommon even in the love of marriage caused him injury I cannot calculate. She grieved for it once, then forgot it, forever and completely. He, on the other hand, played it over in his head twenty times a day for thirty years—though he cherished her all his life. Claude was already born when this happened. They did not reconcile. They did not reconcile until many years later—and Saint was born.

A man, in his heart, left his wife, though he stayed with her in the house, causing dignity—grand, magnificent, and still—to fill the halls and occupy the corridors they tread, for despite himself and anything that he could do, she was what he adored. Then the fruit of reconciliation appeared. His little boy. The issue of their reconciliation, Saint, meant more to Mr. Collier—if possible—than even she whom he adored despite himself. It was Mr. Collier's greatest flaw that he could not forgive her until then.

The slow assurance of his young son's departure from the world accumulated strength as time went on. It threw him off. It threw him off his stately course in life. His boy, to whom he was so attached, had been his treasure, the most solemn gaiety.

One comfort Mr. Collier did not have was religion. His growing interest in lives of the saints was, like his other eccentricities, the refuge and the consolation of the solitary. Some take to the bottle, some look to the sky, but it is all the same. Byzantine empires, lives of the saints? Mr. Collier took to his books, and got overintellectual.

--->≡<---

The Universe As I See It by Albert Einstein lay open on his desk. He was sitting in his chair. I told him about how I got fired, which I had not mentioned before. It was not a small thing to me, that I got fired. He looked at me intently.

"Remember," he said. "Albert Einstein got fired. And as for you, Louise," he said to me again, "you are the artistic one, my dear. Persevere; it suits you."

That is what I mean when I say he was kind.

--->≡<---

It was early in the afternoon. Mr. Collier was in the garden. Mrs. Collier and I sat on the back porch. Mr. Collier was standing under the balcony, looking up at it, then down to the pavement below, the bricks on the side.

He wore ill-fitting khaki pants, old-fashioned sleeveless ribbed undershirts, and white bucks, each article of which was ancient and decrepit, clothes he had had for twenty or thirty years, possibly more than that. He would mutter the Latin names of the trees. Dendrology was consoling to him. He was very big on dendrology. He would take me around the garden and try to interest me in dendrology.

He was a tall man with posture excessively straight, like an arrow. He had a graceful frame, in his stature and in his bearing. He was increasingly thin. His bearing was very stern. He was still dapper when he wore his aging suits and bow ties, cutting quite a figure.

He was just standing there staring at the bricks.

"Don't you think you ought to call him over?" I asked Mrs. Collier. "That's the spot where Saint fell."

"Let him stay," said Mrs. Collier. "It is impossible to distract his mind when he is concentrating."

Mr. Collier stood with his hands in his pockets.

"Maybe it's not a good idea to let him dwell on it like that," I said. "Maybe we should try to strike up a conversation about something normal. Maybe I should call him over."

"No, let him be," she said.

A certain lethargy descended upon the scene.

-->•<--

One day I went to the post office in the pouring rain and while I was standing within the glass door waiting for the rain to let up, I saw Mrs. Collier just sitting there in her car, in the same lethargy. I ran to her car and got in. It poured as we sat there. She said that Mr. Collier had had a nightmare the previous night and that she could not console him, until she led him back to his desk where he was studying the alveolar fricatives of Latin, which she knew would console him, since he found alveolar Latin fricatives very consoling. She said he said that Latin fricatives made life sweet, he knew not why.

-->•<--

Claude called and asked me about his mother.

"She's always crying," he said. "It's different. I've never heard her like this. Every time I talk to her she cries."

"Well, she misses you. I mean, all of a sudden she has an empty house," I said.

"What's going on down there?" Claude persisted. "Is it because of Saint?"

I changed the subject. "So you don't want me to come up there yet?" I said.

"No," he said, in a tiny, quiet, dead voice.

Maybe Claude would break my heart, and it would not really be so outlandish. Hearts have been known to break. Hearts have been known to break before. Maybe he would break my heart, and then I would have Tragic Dignity.

But on the other hand, he would not hurt someone. He was not that kind of person. He didn't consider things from the viewpoint of what they would do for him, or what he would get out of it. That is the first rule of ethics: to guide your conduct by something other than self-interest. There are those who do not understand this, but Claude Collier was not among them.

But I didn't know what Claude was doing now, I only knew in what vicinity he was.

He seemed to be leading a rootless existence.

I could never reach him at his phone. He would just call from those funny-seeming parties, and then he would call from some town on the North Shore of Boston and, even oftener, from Providence. These long distance phone calls continued for some time. I talked to Henry Laines about it, but he was having torments over Mary Grace.

⇥⟩⟨⇤

It was a night in the spring in New York, and the weather had turned fine. A somewhat wastrel but enthusiastic youth was sitting in the lobby of an old hotel, rapidly deteriorating. Namely, Claude Collier. He had the pale-with-zeal look of a young man who has been up late, though whether this was due to nightclubs or insomnia I cannot be entirely sure. Perhaps some harrowing mixture. "I slumber not—the thorn is in my couch"—this was true of him.

His table was strewn with ashtrays, Coke bottles, shredded napkins, and other signs of nervous chaos. In fact, he had not been to nightclubs but had been closeted in the hotel room for three days. He was calmly and obliviously shredding napkins, matchbooks, and cellophane wrappers from cigarette packages, and he had filled about three ashtrays with shreddings.

He was reading a newspaper story about a man in California who "placed sunglasses on his plants to bring out their human features." There was a photograph of a buffoonish-looking elderly man wearing black sunglasses, surrounded by plants also wearing black sunglasses. After studying this concept with the most passionate interest, as though it were the most fascinating piece of news he had seen in a long time and as though people who put sunglasses on their plants were the type with whom he felt most at home, Claude turned to Dr. Joyce Brothers' advice column. Dr. Joyce Brothers reminded him of his mother. They were both always imploring people to take assertiveness-training courses.

He started shredding a new napkin. He ordered another cup of coffee. He had already drunk about fifty-five cups of coffee.

He had just fallen in love with the washroom attendant. Or more accurately, she had just fallen in love with him. The washroom attendant, a voluptuous, fading beauty, was mopping the floor in a narrow side hall of the lobby when Claude walked past.

"Excuse me, doll," she said to him.

"Oh, that's okay, sugar," he said.

She looked at his kind face, and then they stood staring at each other for several moments.

After this rhapsodic encounter, he went back to his seat and shredded more napkins.

Sitting on the other side of him in the overstuffed chairs in the lobby of the old hotel were two little New York girls who were exceedingly bored by everything and whose conversation consisted in cringing in horror at how stupid everyone and everything was. Claude was observing them when a clerk walked through the lobby and began to page him.

He looked up in surprise, and then shredded a few more napkins. The clerk walked through the lobby calling out his page. Finally, Claude sauntered slowly over toward the telephones, as though he thought the race was definitely not to the swift, loitered for a few minutes on the way, engaging in a laconic conversation with the clerk, and then went to the telephone booth and closeted himself in.

It was the Patent Office in Washington, D.C. After staying on the telephone for at least half an hour, Claude Collier nervously walked out of the hotel and took the train to Boston.

•›፠‹•

In Boston, Claude went to some steamship companies and then he went down on the docks and saw the boats, and struck up conversations with the boarding agents. In their offices, he talked to engineers. He went to the Medical School and talked to a physics professor. The professor took him to see an operation so Claude could look at certain instruments. The invention Claude had once patented was not unknown to the professors.

Then he went to the Public Gardens. He went to a bar nearby. He ordered coffee and poured whiskey in it. He drank it while eating fish. He took out a checkbook and some paper and envelopes. He wrote out a check to me, and a letter to his banker, and to the girl at Shell Oil in New Orleans, a friend of his who was looking after the New Levee Well.

•›፠‹•

In New Orleans, I went to my aunts' house and made my arrangements to leave. The night before I left, I just sat around worrying tormentedly about which dresses to pack in my suitcase and which suitcase to bring. I was longing to be gone. But I was wrapped up in my nervous worries. There are always melancholy moments, lugubrious, upon a departure.

•›፠‹•

It was on the train from New York to Boston, one day in the late fall. Sitting next to me on the train was a man from some small town in Tennessee who spoke in weird rural proverbs. He said, "What do you think of me? Tell me, girl, what do you think?"

"I don't know," I said.

"How you know how the jelly tastes till you open the jar?"

Then he cracked up.

He kind of reminded me of Mr. LaSalle at the office—a seriously silly person, on the whole.

Then there was an announcement on the loudspeaker.

"Attention. If there is a Louise Brown on board, please get off the train at New Haven. Louise Brown, get off the train at New Haven. Your party is waiting in New Haven."

"That's me, that's me!" I screamed, breaking my cool exterior. My purse fell on the Tennessee man's head. My bags dropped onto his lap.

"Cat mighty dignified till the dog walk by," he said.

I felt sick. I began to deteriorate. I was a wreck. I had lost my composure.

Standing in the aisle, I said to the Tennessee man, "I'm on the train to Boston and we're almost in New Haven and they called me on the loudspeaker and I'm a nervous wreck and I feel sick."

Then I saw Claude, and I must admit, my heart skipped about twenty beats when I saw him—astounded to see him, the sight of him, which I had lacked for some months. He wore a suit and tie and looked like he was the type of person who worked on Wall Street or something impeccable. He loomed above me on the pavement, above downtown New Haven, everything seeming industrial there. He acted extremely reserved. He looked at me straight with his face in the wind, mild and unintelligible.

"Hi, sweetheart!" he said. (The voice of my beloved.)

❦

We got a cab.

"This girl is tired. Be careful," Claude said to the driver. "She's cold. Close the window."

But about everything else he was evasive. You could not talk to him about anything serious, and I did not even know why we were stopping in New Haven. But we had to go to a science library near the Yale Medical School and consult inventory charts, acting normal and mild and purposeful. Finally, he said, "I was at this party one night, and I dropped a bottle on the floor, like in Texas when I slipped, except the bottle spun around on the floor without breaking, a long-necked bottle pointing toward the North when it dropped, and then I got an idea—" He stopped. "I got another one like the first one. So now I'm in this business."

"What business?" I said.

"For this compass, for this idea I got," he said, remotely apologetic. "I started a company for it."

It was like pulling teeth to get the facts, because he had to shield me from the truth in his rigid rules for the treatment of women.

He wouldn't just sit around and discuss it. He had not mentioned a word of it to his parents or to me, or to anyone, so far as I knew of. But he had invented two compass-like instruments, one a surgical instrument and the other a nautical compass, and he had a little company for them in Cambridge.

❧

It seemed he shortly, however, wanted to develop a new idea, if possible, because he had a new idea, which was an alcohol distiller that would cut the cost in half. Ironically, at least to me, this Collier Distiller was what he was later known for.

On the train, he kept trying to buy me drinks and cigarettes, after leaving New Haven. He had a certain light, gin-like odor about him. We went to the bar on the train and he started joking around with the bartender. They acted like they were having the time of their lives. They had many private jokes.

Then, later, he walked up and down the aisle making friends with all the passengers and doing jokes for them—pretending to fall down on top of them or lunging toward them and saying, "Oh, excuse me," in a riotous tone, like a radio announcer pretending everything is boomingly normal, putting the whole train in a slapstick mood, causing the passengers to believe they were on some sort of a joy ride.

❧

Then we got in a fight.

I said, "Could you please just tone it down a little bit?"

He slumped into his seat. He started shredding matchbooks, slouching gawkily in the seat.

"How is my father?" he said, chewing a straw.

"Well . . ." I considered, then said, "He's fine."

"But how is he really?"

"Fine."

"I don't believe it. He sends me queer letters. My mother cries on the phone."

"They just want to know when you might come home. Maybe they want you to visit."

"I'm just doing my duty. I'm just trying to do my duty."

"But when will you come home, just to visit?" I persisted.

"I don't know," Claude said.

He picked up a napkin and started tearing it into little strips. I just looked at him.

"You just ate a plastic straw, Claude. You swallowed it."

"Okay, well, don't pressure me. Let's all keep calm."

"I'm calm," I said.

"Let's all keep very calm," he said.

"I'M CALM!" I screamed.

He looked at me, his eyes wide with nervousness. In the depths of his eyes was kindness. In his suit and tie, he looked slightly unusual—too old-fashioned, a little stark—in his dark suit, over-starched white shirt, and a sodden, gin-like fragrance as though he had taken too long of a shower.

He got up to get me another drink. He handed me a pack of gum. He went to the café car and bought me Junior Mints.

It was pathetically touching, in a way, how he blindly followed decorum, stoutly, unwaveringly—but something a little desperate in his eyes. If I ever tried to pay him back for something or give him money, he slipped it back into my pocket and gave me a pack of gum or something.

I had an edge on his affections because the longer he had known a person, the better he liked them. He had soft spots for certain people, and always they were those whom he had known the longest in life. Claude Collier would do anything for people like that.

I don't really think loyalty of this kind is very common, because most people have a type of narrow-minded scorn and less fiber than what it takes in a man to constitute loyalty.

Things fade away from most people's hearts. What fades away from their hearts can be ardor, pain, or dignity, it doesn't matter, but it fades away, like the grip of a fist relaxing. But Claude, whose heart was constantly breaking into a million pieces, was different; his grip never relaxed—and that was why he had that air about him, of being attached to someone whom he could not forget.

―≫≡≪―

Then he put on a pair of weird sunglasses and started walking up and down the aisle with his hands in his pockets, patrolling the passengers, otherwise known as his best friends, until we rolled into Back Bay.

He carried my bags to the car. It had been hot on the train and he had taken off his coat. He had become slightly dilapidated on the train. He reminded me of the South. He reminded me of green leaves, gardens, and I loved the way his pants fit. He was still wearing sunglasses, even though it was dark.

On the tape deck in his car he had solo cello suites by Bach. It was a morose kind of music, with the comfort of being pure and austere. But it did not remind me so much of the comical young man I knew; it reminded me of the one who sat in a trance by the tennis courts, listening to opera. People like Claude do not ordinarily listen to morose cello suites. It is not the kind of music they like. It is not of their element—their sociability and lack of solitude, the indiscriminate warmth in their hearts, which is the meaning of generosity. I asked him why he had those morose cello suites on the tape, and he said it was because his heart broke so many times, into a thousand pieces, and that it was constantly doing this.

"You mean your heart's constantly breaking into a million pieces on the floor, like usual, right?"

"I just mean my heart is full—so then I watch it fall on the floor and break into a million pieces. But it's great."

So if you can imagine a person whose heart is constantly breaking but who thinks it is great, then you can understand Claude Collier and his reckless life.

True recklessness is a spirit you do not often see. I suspect it can be exaggerated by drinking. But Claude was never brought up to have caution—yet, for a person whose father had none of the regular vices and practiced moderation in all things, except in books and music, Claude had a blind spot and was inexplicable, in a way, in being a reckless son.

Where did he get it from?

How could he get it in the atmosphere he was brought up in?

—>≡<—

At night, I observed, he drank his gin and listened to Tony Bennett songs. " 'Ohhhh, the good life,' " Claude sang along with Tony Bennett.

Mel came over, that native returned to the North, a person tied to his upbringing, having taken the train too many times from New York to Boston at night with his family when he was little, passing the State House lit in Providence, to be able to give it up.

Mel raved about politics.

Claude listened politely.

—>≡<—

The telephone rang.

"Don't answer it," said Mel.

Claude jumped at the sound of the ring.

"That's right, don't answer it, Louise," said Claude nervously.

They both had looks of terror in their eyes.

"What is the matter with you two?" I said.

"Don't answer it," Mel commanded.

"Don't answer it, Louise," repeated Claude.

We just sat in his room with the phone ringing. The room was littered with blueprints. The apartment showed signs of Claude's personal trademarks, such as an ashtray emptied onto the bed, and his "filing system," which was a closet full of suits with scraps of paper sticking out of the pockets.

Another area of concern was the mailbox, as it was Claude's habit to read his mail while standing at the mailbox and then simply put it back in.

"This place is a mess," I said.

"No, it's organized in a special way," said Claude.

But "Life was sweet, I knew not why"—so we just sat there listening to the cornball Tony Bennett songs.

--◦≫⊞≪◦--

In the mornings he seemed frail and ate very cautiously.

"It hurts to eat," he said. He ate just enough to work up to the first cigarette of the day.

If he was making a business call on the telephone, he would pace about the room while talking and get all tangled up in the wire, absent-minded, oblivious, and intent.

He played football with Mel, who had a team. They played on a field by the Harvard stadium, across from the Business School. I sat on a bench in dark shadows and an almost cloying scent in the air, as though it were gardenia.

Claude had on a wrinkled over-large navy blue T-shirt and over-large corduroy pants, his clothes several sizes too large even on his tall frame.

I was unable to look at any other on the field. I could not focus on them clearly. They were just blurred Yankees in T-shirts on a field.

I must, as ever, return to New Orleans, I thought.

--◦≫⊞≪◦--

We drove to Providence, where there was a political lecture, with deck chairs set outside the City Hall. On the colonial hill where the university was, there was another lecture on the green by a journalist. It was all earnest and sober. The Yankees were upright and full of concern, talking about politics. They had great energy. Claude dreaded them in a way, because in comparison he felt like a crackpot, and they made him want to drink, to become even more of a crackpot.

--◦≫⊞≪◦--

We went on to Newport, R.I., a place more beautiful, of course, than many another, the clear cold ardor on the cliffs.

"You see that school?" Claude said. "St. George's. That is where I would have sent Saint."

We drove down a road with low stone walls and maple trees, his morose solo cello suites blaring away in the night. The cold air was enough to break your heart, with the mansions brooding on the cliffs. The cold air broke my heart, it was so upright and stern. I was happy then. With him I had a taste of humanity.

However, he was not well. At the time.

In the mornings, he sat in his bathrobe watching television, smoking cigarettes, blueprint diagrams spread out on his lap and all over the floor. He would always be in his bathrobe, drinking a glass of soda and lime—working on his blueprints, chewing a straw.

Often he had visitors. He was not well, but very few people felt that. The telephone rang very often with calls from New Orleans, old friends of his who were accustomed to call him every day in life, who did not seem to feel right unless they could talk to him.

Sometimes, he would sit in this old bathrobe looking at a picture book of Italy where they had taken Saint, pointing out the places he had shown him. And then every once in a while Claude would look at you and look as though straight through you and as though he had forgotten who you were.

--)BK(--

One night we were driving home and he was making jokes and laughing so hysterically that he had to stop the car and go stand outside and laughed until he cried. The next minute, a look came into his eyes, and he said, "I'm not feeling too well. I don't think I can drive. The fact is, Louise, just get me home."

He was a nervous wreck. He slumped in his seat, silent, until we got home. Once inside the house he said, "Wait—did you hear that?"

"What?"

"Listen. You didn't hear anything? I think it's some robbers at the back door."

"There's nothing," I said. "Just go to bed."

"Wait, I better go check. You stay here. Don't move."

There was nothing there.

He lay on his bed shaking like a leaf. It was the same as his father with his troubles, I think. I don't know what it was, a person without comfort.

The telephone rang.

"Don't answer it," Claude said.

—⟫✠⟪—

"Louise!" Claude screamed from the bathroom. "Okay, Louise, come brush your teeth! I have your toothbrush ready! Come on, time to get up! I've been sitting in here for a half hour fixing everything up for you! Come on! Your toothbrush is ready, it's waiting for you!"

In the bathroom, two toothbrushes were lined up on the sink, each one piled about two inches high with toothpaste. I smiled politely at Claude, who was sitting on the rim of the bathtub trying to suppress hysterical mirth.

—⟫✠⟪—

His company was in a small industrial-looking building on Broadway in Cambridge with a very, very small silver plate by the door that said Collier Instruments. I glimpsed the reception room at the front of the office, which contained two middle-aged secretaries, one wearing red velour bell-bottoms and the other with a beehive hairdo, one known as Miss Agnes and the other known as Lucille.

It seemed preposterous to me that these two ladies would have such a young man for their boss, but who worshiped the ground he walked on for the dignity and sweetness of his behavior and that he piled on them many compliments, and who would watch him when he came in late, or who would not watch him when he did not come in at all, or who would offer timid imprecations when he staggered in pale and stark, or who would watch him come in at seven in the morning wearing sunglasses, his rash youth, and a look of drunken splendor.

—⟫✠⟪—

"What did you do for lunch," he said, "while I was gone."

"I don't know."

"What do you mean, you don't know?"

"I don't know, a cheese sandwich or something."

"A cheese sandwich? You had a cheese sandwich?" he said, mystified.

"Yes, Claude, I had a cheese sandwich."

"You mean, you just went into the kitchen at around noon and fixed a cheese sandwich?" he asked.

"Yes, Claude," I said.

"It's so sweet, you just going into the kitchen to fix a cheese sandwich."

"I know. It's heartbreaking. Your heart's probably breaking into a million pieces on the floor right now."

"What kind of cheese?" he resumed absently, with his ridiculous and relentless curiosity for small concrete facts. "Louise, you have to eat right," he said, looking at me attentively. "You have to take care of yourself."

"I'M NOT THE ONE WHO CAN'T TAKE CARE OF HIMSELF!" I screamed.

He stared. "Let's all keep calm, Louise," he said. "Keep calm. There's no reason to raise your voice. There's never any reason for a person to raise his voice above a normal speaking tone."

Lord give me strength, I whispered to the ceiling.

"You should lead a regulated life, Louise. That's what you need, Louise."

"*What about you?*"

"What do you mean?"

"Why don't *you* do that, Claude?"

"But I already do. That *is* what I do. I'm just a normal, boring guy. I'm just a boring guy, Louise."

"Cut that out."

"No one could be more normal than me," he continued. "I get up, I go to the office, I sit behind a desk all day. Louise, I'm just a normal, boring guy."

--)BK(--

We went to the opera. The whole time, during the most beautiful parts of the music, Claude kept saying, "What does it all mean? What does he mean by that? What is he trying to say, do you think? What does it all mean?"

He had packed my purse with Junior Mints beforehand.

--)BK(--

There was a famous old judge at the opera from the Massachusetts Supreme Court who befriended us at intermission. He was an expert on jurisprudence. He was the world expert on jurisprudence, and had taught at Oxford for many years before returning to his native Boston. He wore a bow tie and carried a cane. He had known Mr. Collier at law school and college, and they had been on a committee together in Washington for Franklin Roosevelt. The judge said Mr. Collier was the only one of the committee who stuck to his guns. He said he was the only honest member. Mr. Collier had been twenty-nine at the time, twenty-nine years old and the most honest one on this committee for Franklin Roosevelt. Claude kept telling the judge that it was a privilege to meet him, and the judge would say, "No, it's a privilege to meet the son of Louis Collier." The judge said to Claude, "Your father means more to me than I have words to say."

~✦~

It was two weeks later that we received the telegram, FATHER NERVOUS BREAKDOWN COME HOME.

~✦~

Mr. Collier sat in his library all day while his limbs jumped and shook. He played the "Hallelujah Chorus" on an elaborate tape machine, at full blast, the first thing upon waking up in the morning. He requested his wife to turn off the air-conditioner and keep all the windows in the house, all the shutters, wide open—the "Hallelujah Chorus" spread throughout the Garden District as a backdrop to the monumental palms silhouetted, raging, against the twilight sky. The "Hallelujah Chorus" blared throughout the block, and he read Shelley:

> Though thou art ever fair and kind,
> The forests ever green,
> Less oft is peace in Shelley's mind
> Than calm in waters seen.

~✦~

The large families populating Perseverance and Souvenir, his plantations in Vermillion Parish, as well as family and friends and retainers in New Orleans, relied on Mr. Collier. It was his role to protect them, whose holdings were undisclosed in hidden assets in mineral rights and in shares of the Louisiana Bank, whose holdings were grounded in the same. Due to the customary retrograde, eccentric, tomb-like silence of the Bank, regulated by state charter and the Napoleonic Code, to avoid disclosure with the Federal Reserve, Mr. Collier had to guard the Bank from takeovers and protect the leases of the dependents in his entourage. These undisclosed holdings in Louisiana land were tied up with his affairs and the affairs of those others whom he protected, friends and family, which were many. While his ruined sugar plantations decayed on plots surrounded by oil refineries, and as his swamplands lay smoldering above nascent Sunbelt prosperity, these interests fell onto Claude's shoulders.

Mr. Collier was born on the plantation of his forebears in Louisiana. His great-grandfather was a peddler. A Jew, he left Germany for Louisiana in 1836, at a time when the Jews had just been granted the right to own property, which they were formerly denied and which in neighboring parts they were still denied. But he left, anyway, with a fair volume of others. Still, a Jew can't flee persecution no matter where he goes, though it seemed melancholy that he left anyway, Mr. Collier's ancestor, as though out of pride. He would not accept favors from his persecutors. He was, like Mr. Collier, stern and unforgiving. The ancient blood of the Jews coursed in his veins from dark Germany.

Then he married a French Catholic girl in Vermillion Parish in Louisiana, in whose veins coursed the gay, light-hearted blood of those who had founded Louisiana in the name of Louis, roi de France.

They represented the two types of humanity—the frivolous and the grave.

Owning property was exactly what Mr. Collier's ancestor wanted to do, as it turned out, as that is what he did in Louisiana, where he acquired two plantations—Perseverance and Souvenir—and after the War, others.

They moved to New York, I can't make out exactly why, and left their property tied up in the South.

It appeared they would give up the South, I can't make out exactly why.

But when the War came, they returned. Not, however, for sympathy with the cause, but for business reasons. He was very keen on his property. The tenants fled or were ruined, and he had to preserve his property. All his family's future prosperity, it owed to the South.

He just wanted to look after his family.

He went back to Perseverance, where Mr. Collier was born.

They built up a modest empire in that parish, for planting sugar was not what it once was. They also acquired property in the Rigolets, Lake Borgne, and the Chef Menteur Pass. They built the levees, which were indispensable, due to the low elevation and tropical storms. Mr. Collier and his six brothers went off to Harvard from the obscure plantation in Louisiana, and when they returned, oil was discovered on the property.

--》圈《--

Mr. Collier sat in his study and fingered a ring which his wife had not worn for many years. He gave it to her when they married. She returned it to him one day in the late fall of 1950, and they did not reconcile until Saint was conceived.

The ring was a thin gold band carved with vines. On the inside it was inscribed *I Cling To Thee.*

--》圈《--

All he wanted to do was think about Byzantine empires and be closeted in his house and study obscure pedantic details. All he ever did was listen to the "Hallelujah Chorus" at full volume, and sometimes he would venture out into the garden, with the "Hallelujah Chorus" blaring, and listen to it there, muttering in Latin or in ancient Greek, in his bathrobe there.

Otherwise than that he was pedantic, he was a simple man, who spoke in simple platitudes, was down-to-earth, and, like his son, could get on with all types of people and had time for them despite that he had been a terribly busy man, was one who would stop to be solicitous and kind. Perseverance, industry, and honor, these were his simple credos, to which he rigidly adhered.

But standing in the garden there at night, listening to the "Hallelujah Chorus," he was like an apparition. The "Hallelujah Chorus," it was what he could thoroughly understand. It was of his element. It was made of the same stuff he was.

He was an innocent. What he heard in the worship of the chorus was not God. What he believed in was the exaltation of the chorus, for his mate, his wife—that is what he heard in it. It was the same as when he had heard it with her when she was a college girl in Boston—to him it was no different. There is only one thing such inarticulate radiance, exaltation, can describe, and that was your conjugal faith, a heavenly mansion raging in the dark.

⇥✦⇤

It was raining and stormy and green. I felt like I was in France.

I always felt like I was in France, along the rainy boulevards.

It rained every day. It was always gray, and nothing could be more consoling, more gentle and mild. Claude viewed the city after having left it for over a year—overgrown and green, hauntingly, sometimes discouragingly, familiar.

⇥✦⇤

It was the day of the Kentucky Derby—May fourth, I believe. On Claude's desk were some invitations to parties in Louisville that week.

"I have to call my friend in Louisville," he said.

He said on the wire: "Here's the tip—Fearless Contessa."

He listened on the wire.

In his room I found a list of horses.

Boudoir Attire
First Mistake
Home In Paris
Raise Your Ante
Seaside Flirt
War Flirt
Tropic King
Hilarious
Saint I Ain't

⇥✦⇤

We went to the country to Perseverance and Souvenir. The grace of Perseverance set a calm into my heart—the famous avenue of oaks, the gardenia and banana trees. We sat on wrought-iron chairs painted green, looking out to the avenue of oaks. The men wore seersucker suits and horn-rimmed glasses and the matriarchs were the salt of the earth who exhibited untold charm and mirth through such adversities as seven pregnancies, as though it were their duty to be gay, made life a dancing matter for those about them, who also behaved in the exact same way.

The sons hunted duck and alligator in the bayou behind the house. The men in seersucker suits and white linen suits mopped their brows in the heat, but did not take off their coats. A private plane flew in for the annual meeting and banquet of stockholders. Claude became riotous. When we were separated at the banquet, he suddenly grew despondent, then lethargic, then passed out under the porch.

On the way home, I toured the gardens of Souvenir while he slept in the car. He woke up suddenly.

"You're meeting someone there, aren't you?" he raved. "You're meeting someone later! You're meeting a lover there!"

Naturally, this was such a preposterous concept that I couldn't even really frame it in my mind. He was always full of hare-brained schemes that he thought people did. To him, the world was this huge den of iniquity where people did wild ruinous things.

Then we passed the Bonnet Carre Spillway and he suddenly grew scientific. He started discussing the levee construction, which lets the waters of the Mississippi, when they get too high, run into Lake Pontchartrain. He stopped and looked at it with binoculars and discussed types of waves. He looked at it for about an hour and a half.

Then he went home and closeted himself in his room for three days. It was filled with blueprints and bottles. The mail brought letters from oil companies. He had many visitors. There would at times be a line in the hall, ranging from his old friends in olive drab suits and bow ties, to his old friends, wino lunatics, to his new friends, oil-lease dependents.

No one will ever know how many people he helped.

No one will ever know, however, too, some of the shady people and things he was mixed up with.

Then, when they were gone, he closeted himself in his room again, or went to weird racetrack dives.

—>≈<—

The telephone rang. Claude, as a matter of habit, looked up in terror. No matter how many people he helped, it still filled him with a certain amount of basic terror.

It was a call from Louisville.

In the evening paper, there was a story about a racetrack scandal. At the end of the story, there was a list of bettors who had been big winners on the horses. Included was Claude Collier. There were about thirty names. When he came back from the phone call, I handed him the story. He read it slowly and thoroughly, standing up.

"God," he said quietly.

—>≈<—

The doorbell rang. It was a detective calling to see Claude.

"Oh God," Claude said.

He forged downstairs, knowing only one way to handle it.

They sat downstairs in the study, and closed the doors. They were together at least an hour. Toward the end of the hour, I could hear laughter and guffaws coming from their quarter. Then, when Claude showed the detective to the door, they were smoking cigars and acting like brothers or best friends.

"Don't forget me, Hal," said Claude.

"You can count on it, babe—except downtown," said the detective.

When the man left, Claude stared at the door in utter dismay.

—>≈<—

I sat in the study with Mr. Collier, who was reading a book that was written in some wholly unrecognizable language that was a mixture of ancient characters and mathematical symbols. Byron was negotiating imaginary screeching racing-car turns at his feet.

Byron screeched to a halt before Mr. Collier. Mr. Collier fell to pieces around small children. Small children made him get an uncanny smile and caused him to fall into bemusement.

"What have we here?" he said to Byron.

He looked at him gently.

"A rascal," said Mr. Collier.

He looked away, a high-minded, philosophical look on his face.

The doorbell rang. Mrs. Stewart the elder came doddering in.

"How are you, Alice?" said Mr. Collier.

"My trunks are packed. I'm ready," she said.

"Oh? Where are you going?"

"I leave that to the Lord," she said. Then she described her old beaux.

—·❦❦·—

Mr. Walter Stewart also came.

"Don't you know your son is in very hot water?" said Mr. Stewart to Mr. Collier.

"In what sense, Walter?" said Mr. Collier.

—·❦❦·—

Claude was pacing the floor, his expression nervous, chewing a pencil.

"Louise. Louise. Louise," he was saying under his breath, not thinking, as though in a pattern, while he paced, as though an involuntary reflex.

I walked in and looked at him.

"Oh," he said. "Louise. Louise," he said. "So it's you, just standing there—perfect. Louise, why are you so perfect?"

"No one is perfect, Claude," I said judiciously.

—·❦❦·—

"Claude," said Mrs. Collier, coming in, wringing her hands, "there's a man on the phone who says his name is immaterial and he's making a conference call from Louisville."

Claude was gone a long time on the telephone. Meanwhile, the doorbell rang. It was the detective who had called on Claude the previous day. He wore an uncomfortable look. Claude came in shortly and they closeted themselves in the downstairs study again.

It was dark and breezy and impending rain. Then I heard Claude singing in the downstairs hall, and striding up the stairs. He came striding up the stairs, bellowing out his crazy 1920s jazz songs. I stood in the doorway, and he stood there looking at me in the way he had, as though he had forgotten some question he had wanted to ask.

-->)BK(--

That night we just sat out on the balcony until it got light again. It must have been for about eight hours, just sitting there. The birds started singing before midnight, like some tropical rain forest in Africa. Claude talked the entire time about Lucille, his secretary in Boston, and Chester, and later transferred to small lame-brained concrete details of my daily routine and the wonder of my general existence. He chain-smoked Tareytons.

We looked out to the garden. It was balmy. He gave me to understand some things about his condition. It is amazing to me how bad some people can be, and yet seem so stunningly good, their kisses like angels, breathtaking innocence. His kisses were like the entire state of Louisiana, and Mississippi also, on a fresh old day, also representing many generations, and taught me anything I may know of humanity. So if they taught me that, I will leave it to your imagination what the rest taught me.

"I'm nuts about you, kid. I'm coconuts about you," said Claude.

In the morning we were still just sitting there, like two insane people. There was some movement in the street, black women wearing turbans on their heads, red Cadillacs passing by with disco music blaring out the window. It was like the early morning in some provincial town near the equator, with a hot, lethargic charm, and somehow an air of corruption, which was mixed with the innocence of life in the provinces, in a small town. An uncanny mixture, it was the fateful green garden of my youth.

-->)BK(--

We drove down the Avenue—it was like France—a boulevard, with oak trees at regular intervals, a roof of branches and leaves—in the debauched soggy morning to my house. It was breezy and dark and impending rain, as the old Avenue raged.

There was a screen porch at the front of my apartment which looked onto the Avenue, in which the streetcar rumbled past, against the unending green. This provided scenes of arresting beauty with the madcap palm trees raging against the twilight sky so that I often was transfixed there, on the screen porch, looking to the Avenue.

Claude was pacing around the room shredding napkins and matchbooks and piercing little holes in cellophane wrappers with a fountain pen. Then he passed out. Before that, he was listening to weird Arabian dance music on the radio. I turned it off. I sat on the screen porch in the green, being arrested by scenes of arresting beauty.

The telephone rang. "I'll get it," said Claude in a dead voice from the floor.

"Coroner's office," he said into the phone in a dead voice.

He said it was Henry Laines. "He wants us to come over," he said.

So we went back down the Avenue, being arrested by scenes of arresting beauty, to Henry's house, with his paintings of carnival balls, the queens and debutantes and men in white tie and tails in ominous, morbid, gay rows.

--➤✠✦--

Henry was engaged in his favorite pastime, which was spying on the neighbors. The Stewarts' mansion, with all its inner chaos, could be viewed from his back gallery, across several gardens.

It was shortly after his first wedding anniversary. He was furious. They had fought. Evidence of his wrath lay on the floor, pots and pans and suitcases.

Mary Grace was having a birthday, her twenty-ninth. She was having a party, in Mississippi in the town on the Gulf near Bay St. Louis, at her family's house, where we used to go as children. I would not like to relive my childhood there—for among its inner chaos and the young marrieds (everyone's parents) and screaming children strewn in corners of grandiose lawns, Ruthie Legendre had a nervous breakdown because her husband was a playboy, and neither were the Colliers uninvolved.

Henry showed us the invitation. The invitation was on a hot pink filing card with a quote from F. Scott Fitzgerald, something about a woman of twenty-nine is the same as a girl of nineteen, no more bears in the closet for either one.

"Whatever that means," said Henry Laines. "She's in one of her moods," he said.

"When is it?" I said.

"When is what?"

"The party?"

"Oh. It's today. Tonight. Right now. It's right now," Henry Laines said.

"Are you kidding?" said Claude. "Come on, boy. We're going. We're going right now."

⬩⟩▒⟨⬩

Whenever I pass through Waveland, Mississippi, I think of Little Egypt, which is the plantation where I first met Claude. It was owned by the Stewarts, who conducted their emotional crises there. When I was little, we used to go there, with the young marrieds, the parents. Ruthie and Sully Legendre would drink all day and night by the pool—sex, an air of sex, old-fashioned bathing suits and black 1950s sunglasses with weird pointy frames, loud sexy music on the record player with saxophones, and the maid saying that afternoon to Mrs. Legendre, "He don't mean nuthin by it, Miss Ruthie. Take him back."

And the letter he wrote which I found in a drawer, asking her to take him back, begging her to. He was a playboy, Mr. Legendre, he was wild. He used to be best friends with Mr. Collier, but the Colliers never often went to Little Egypt. It was not their kind of place—with that loud sexy saxophone music playing by the pool all the time, while the young marrieds danced.

Mr. and Mrs. Legendre were the raciest ones.

Mrs. Collier, a Yankee suddenly in Mississippi, watched them in amazement.

Mrs. Legendre had a nervous breakdown, and they had to drag her screaming from the Gulf. It was during a carnival parade—which they also have in Mississippi along the Gulf—everyone in their costumes. And yet the maid said, in that one sultry slow moment of time, "He don't mean nuthin by it, Miss Ruthie. Don't let him go."

A stony silence descended on the place, and I would not like to relive that part of my childhood. The world stopped then—the Little Egypt of the wild young marrieds, the playboy father, the black maids, the children screaming in toy cars on lawns, their mothers with pointy black sunglasses, their laughter late at night. The world stopped—it was terrible and sad—and they didn't dance by the pool all day and night anymore with that loud sexy music. A stony silence then descended on the place. Little Egypt was from then on sad and mysterious, whereas those people had not been sad and mysterious, they had been full of life.

Mrs. Legendre was a Texas belle. She was violently beautiful. She would say things like, "What are you in this business for except love?"

She was like Mary Grace Stewart—one minute she was the life of the party, and the next minute her head was in her hands and she had to be led, weeping, from the place. She had a lot of Breakdowns.

Some irretrievable thing between them all in the love of marriage, dating from Little Egypt, gave that nameless sadness to the place—grand, magnificent, and still.

--❧--

But you could not take the sheer grandeur from the place, the madcap palms, the fading Mississippi glamour which, to me, its former inhabitants still had.

--❧--

Little Egypt was abandoned. The house was in disarray. There was a note from Mary Grace to the effect that the party had moved on.

--❧--

Claude was driving, racing along the highway like a maniac.

We got pulled over for speeding.

The officer came to the window and said to Claude, "What's the rush, son?"

"No rush, sir," said Claude.

"Where's the fire?" the officer continued.

"No fire," Claude said.

Claude got out of the car and put his arm around the officer, and they walked a few paces off, looking at the Gulf. Henry Laines, who was slumped dejectedly in the back seat, rolled his eyes heavenward.

Claude and the officer were standing by some leaning palms on the beach. They were having the time of their lives. The officer had to take off his sunglasses and wipe tears from his eyes. Finally, they returned, shook hands warmly, and parted with regret. Then we prepared to drive on, except the car wouldn't start. Claude went out onto the road, flailing his arms. Someone stopped and had jumper cables. But the motor died again about fifty feet after that.

"Let's get a drink," said Claude.

--➤✦❦✦←--

The famous Mississippi camellias were in bloom. We walked to the macabre Mirror Lounge of the Palmetto Inn, which was populated by a group of toothless old men. A mysterious toothless man kept buying me beers. The waitress kept bringing me beers, ones I did not order. I would say, "Oh, I'm sorry—I didn't order a beer," and she would smile and point to the bar behind her, where there was a row of grinning, toothless old men.

I appeal to toothless old men. To toothless old men, I am particularly appealing. The bar was filled with grotesque old men, wrecks and grotesques, the type I appeal to, and the type Claude loved.

"Can I read?" I said to Claude, taking out my copy of *The Universe As I See It* by Albert Einstein, lent to me by Mr. Collier.

"Can she read?" Claude asked the bartender and the grotesque old men all around. "Can she read? Do you mind if she reads?" he said in his deadpan. He went over and conferred with the toothless old men. They were the key to the universe as Claude Collier saw it.

An ancient black man started playing the piano. My companion, with his certain Southern kindness, got this ancient black man over to our table.

Clarence Puglia.

Claude knew him. He was a jazz piano player from New Orleans.

"Come over here, baby," said Claude to Clarence Puglia after he finished his set.

Clarence Puglia told all his stories, about how Clarence Puglia would never be famous because he didn't leave town and didn't sell himself or promote himself or be opportunistic, when it was he who was the best. Later he started telling dirty jokes which sent him and other members of my party, even Henry Laines, into paroxysms of mirth. Finally we got a taxi and left, with Clarence Puglia an addition to our party.

⁎⁓⧁⧀⧁⧀⁓⁎

We got to a bar along the Mississippi coast in one of the small towns. It was a country bar, right on the Gulf, and the entire clientele looked like it had just stepped out of law school, with horn-rimmed glasses predominant. The band was playing old songs from that 1960s era in which New Orleans and environs remain, even though it is twenty years later. They're just always playing old songs where I live.

Mary Grace was on the dance floor, gripped in the torrid embrace of her old flame, Tom.

Claude took a seat with Henry and me in a corner. A thin young black man wearing white beach pants and a Hawaiian shirt sidled over to me and started singing. He just looked at me and started singing while dancing obliviously to the band, and got my hand and started dancing, pulling me toward the floor.

"Ride the pony, girl," he said.

"What?" I said.

"Ride the pony, girl," he persisted, dancing around.

"No—uh—I can't," I said loudly.

"Ride the pony, girl," he continued to repeat, in his trance on the dance floor.

"*I can't,*" I said again loudly. "I just—can't."

--⟩⬛⟨--

I went back to our table. Someone had taken my chair, and there was no room at the table. I sat down on a high seat at the bar.

A large, beefy young man, with horn-rimmed glasses, weaved purposefully in my direction, and propelled himself into my lap—he actually sat down on my lap. I tried to heave him off, but his weight was too great.

"Baby!" he said.

All I could do was sit there. "*What are you doing?*" I said. Then he just got up, as though nothing had happened, and wandered off into the crowd, his head tilted optimistically toward some unknown point across the dance floor, his expression rapturous.

The bartender was a strange specimen of humanity who you couldn't tell if he was a man or a woman, but he had a plastic name tag which said Caesar. His hair had a strange pompadour. He started trying to strike up a conversation, and winked at me. I don't know why but I am the type of person who, I'll be minding my own business walking down the street, say, and suddenly I'll realize that some wrecked kind of a person is following along behind me at a discreet distance, like a grinning toothless old man, or a gawking horn-rimmed law student, or a person named Caesar, who you can't tell if he is a man or a woman, or someone like that will corner me at a bar and start trying to tell me All Their Problems, or help me with mine. Actually, it often adds a certain comic relief to my life, for which I am grateful—but, on the other hand, it kind of gets on my nerves.

Claude would like to spend his whole life with people like that.

--⟩⬛⟨--

Henry was asking Claude about New York.

"New York reminds me of popular songs," said Claude.

"What?"

"I mean, in New Orleans you listen to old songs or outmoded

songs or old-time jazz; but in New York you listen to popular songs. It's more American than New Orleans."

"You hated New York, didn't you, Mary Grace?" said Henry.

"No, I loved New York," she said.

"You're in one of your moods," Henry said. "You know you hated New York."

"You're in one of *your* moods," she said.

"Moods? One of my moods? I'm not in one of my moods. This is me. This is my personality. I don't have moods. You're in one of *your* moods."

"Men don't have moods," said Claude.

--)≡(--

Claude went over to the dance floor and accidentally knocked over a waitress with a tray of drinks. They went sprawling toward the floor together when he tried to help her up. Then he tried to make a big joke out of it. He appeared to be deteriorating. He was drinking an untold amount of gin and seemed on the brink of decrepitude. But unaccountably, though a man like that will always seem on the brink of decrepitude, he will never go over the brink to decrepitude, never quite. Instead, he has a curious freshness, a curiously upright posture, he is a total enigma, with that formal stiff upright posture. In him, you will find at fifty, say, the rare vitality of one blue-eyed fifty-year-old man with a bow tie that is in itself one sight enough to make life worth living.

He was talking to a girl I heard some things about from the time before Henry Laines' wedding when I did not see much of Claude. It was only at the time of Henry Laines' wedding when he gave Henry that funny, inscrutable stare from across the dance floor and when he held my collar, that I began to get my glimpse of humanity. There was this dignity Claude had.

"Louise, Louise," he would say in his odd reflex, unthinking, trying to steady himself. He did the same with Saint's name—he would find himself repeating the name.

The night bore on. The last I saw of Claude was when the debauchees drove past an old restaurant where we later went in a black limousine with champagne glasses, along the Gulf among the old oaks and Spanish moss, the essential debauchee alone in the huge back seat, a sharp picture of that vulgar decadence. The car stopped in the black, glamorous night with a mild summer breeze in front of the restaurant and then drove along the Gulf with the "Blue Danube" blaring.

⇥⃛⬧⃛⇤

At five o'clock in the morning, my telephone rang. It was Claude, calling from jail. He said he was calling from jail.

I went down to Central Lock-Up, where they kept the prisoners, among them, Claude. He was wearing what once was a khaki suit, tennis shoes, and what was once a tie. However, he looked like his father. He was talking to a hardened criminal in his cell. He was chewing a straw. He was staring intently at the hardened criminal's face. He seemed perfectly sober.

I brought him home. When we got to his house, there was a letter from the lawyer and a summons for him to appear in court a month hence to be questioned in the racehorse case.

That night he had to go to Night Court to answer the charge of Public Drunk.

⇥⃛⬧⃛⇤

We drove down Broad Street and passed a church with its doors wide open. Inside were seven elderly black men wearing gray polyester suits and dark sunglasses, with white hair, singing gospel music on a stage set up with microphones and amplifiers, snapping their fingers—namely, the Zion Harmonizers. They could be heard up and down the street. Next door to the church was a bar, Comeaux's, Grits Comeaux, Prop., with bare light bulbs outside shining onto huge stacks of newspapers with little boys who were trying to collect stacks that had fallen into the street. It was the Ninth Ward, with Creole cottages with shuttered doors and dormer windows, and people of varying shades of brown colors, and uncharacteristically treeless streets.

At Night Court, everyone sat in rows in a room with a closed-off space next to the judge's bench where the hardened criminals had to sit barricaded off by themselves, after being conducted through a special entrance leading directly from the jail, which was adjacent to the criminal courts.

The hardened criminals had to file out one by one with their names called out. They weaved their way to their seats.

There were bright orange signs posted at frequent intervals reading NO SMOKING BY ORDER OF THE LOUISIANA FIRE MARSHAL. Everyone was chain-smoking.

Claude sat calmly in his chair. Several of his cohorts had come down to see his case be tried, and sat a few rows behind us, talking laconically among themselves. Claude wasn't called to the bench until one-thirty in the morning, when he pled guilty and paid a fifteen-dollar fine.

He conducted himself very mildly.

But when we got outside, the laconic young men in their seersucker suits came up and took him away. "He needs sympathy," they said. "We'll help him recuperate." One of them produced a pint of Wild Turkey from his coat pocket and let out a yell.

I was standing there, staring at Claude. He returned the scrutiny. I looked at him surrounded by his cronies, standing on the Avenue—that expanse of green arched over with venerable oaks—and I could plainly see that despite anything, Claude Collier was a desperate character. I do not know what made him that way, but he was.

—⟩▣⟨—

It was Sunday afternoon, pouring down rain. I went to Claude's house to pick him up; we were going to eat in the Quarter. Everything was wet and dark green in the Garden District. There was an intensity to life. I went into his room. He was hurriedly knotting his tie, moving around his cluttered room with diagrams piled up on the floor, the rain sliding off the banana trees outside his window and into the room. He was wearing his black suit. He was worriedly going around the room trying to finish getting dressed, acting curiously shy, and there was in his demeanor firmly cast, something logical and wry.

"Keep calm," he said, rushing around.

"I *am* calm," I said.

"Let's all keep calm," he said, knotting his tie.

On Chartres Street, there was the sweet dark greenness, every-thing quiet and Cuban and French in the Quarter. It was pouring down rain.

We went to the corner of Bourbon and Iberville, where the line outside the restaurant for people waiting to get in had stretched all along the sidewalk to the corner. On Bourbon Street, there were throngs of people, even on Sunday afternoon—tourists, whores, drunks, toothless old men, strippers, bouncers, jazz in the streets.

We stood waiting in line.

The men called out, "Hey, baby, c'mere!" and some small black boys were tap dancing next to someone who chanted:

> *Quarter red beans, quarter rice,*
> *Little piece of salt meat to make it taste nice.*
> *Give me a reefer and a gang of gin—*
> *No one knows the state I'm in.*

The inside of the restaurant was one dazzling blast of light—bulbs and white tile. A thin horizontal mirror ran all the way around the single rectangular room, light bulbs bounding it above and below at short intervals, and above that a strip of dark green upholstery with stately black umbrellas hanging from hooks. It was dazzlingly light, with the bulbs and the white tile, the grandiose chandeliers. The waiters wore tuxedos and all lounged around a dark mahogany bureau in the back of the room.

The atmosphere was humid, and I fell into something of a daze. The tables were filled with old judges, society men, their vivacious wives.

Claude had cocktails. The waiter brought a telephone to our table. He whispered something to Claude. "All right, okay," said Claude softly, and then the waiter said something else quietly into his ear. Claude looked at him in astonishment, wide-eyed, mute.

Then he picked up the receiver, listened, and spoke into the telephone softly, softly. After a few minutes, he nodded, said something else in a tiny, quiet, dead voice, and hung up.

"Who was that?" I said wildly.

"Come on," he said quietly.

"Who was it?" I said.

"It was a friend of mine," Claude said. "I think it looks like I'll have to talk to him after we eat. Just a friend of mine. I think I'll just have to send you home by yourself after this, though."

He started shredding a napkin. Then he stopped. "I'll work it out," he said with finality.

I just looked at him. "I'm exhausted," I said, "I need rest."

"Yes!" he said rather wildly. "You need rest. You certainly do. I can really understand how much rest you need. Rest. I've been very worried about you. Thank God you're all right. You need rest. You have to take care of yourself. You have to be careful."

"Okay, okay, okay."

"You shouldn't spread yourself too thin, Louise. Socializing is totally meaningless. You pick up mannerisms from people and get all fake and affected from being too social. You should not be too social. You should go home and study. You should just follow the straight and narrow path. The other thing I would tell you is this—open your heart, open your heart. My father told me that, way back when. Everything is completely useless if you don't do that. I can't see any humanity in you if you don't open your heart. Everyone out there is just kind of dumb in the heart. I don't want you to be like that."

"Why do you have to be involved in all these shady things?" I said. "Who are you going to meet? Why do you have to get dragged down by all these shady things? You're so good."

"Louise, you pick the wrong person to idolize," he said softly, squinting at the table. Then he looked at me gently. "You have said many pleasant things about me, heart, but I am not the person you portray." He stopped. "But that is unimportant. The important thing is that you felt like saying them. You talk about my heart—you are my heart," he said. "And there you are, just sitting there like everything is completely normal. Isn't your neck cold? You must be freezing. You didn't even bring an umbrella. And there you are, just sitting there like everything is completely normal."

"Well, what do you expect me to do—get up on the table and

start dancing, because you are all embroiled in all these shady things and I don't even know what they are?"

"Don't worry," he said. "Don't worry. I can handle it. I'll have to."

He would not tell me what it was, or where he was going. He had to shield me from the truth, because that was his rigid rule. I knew he was going off to be embroiled in shady catastrophic dealings and ruinous involvements, which did not fit into his character, and yet which were steadfast there. I could have kept on asking him to tell me what it was, or I could have said nothing, which is what I did.

When we left and came back onto Bourbon, it being the height of the tourist season, it was astonishingly wild. The street stretched down past view in the night, everything honky-tonk and degenerate.

"Be careful," I said.

He stood in his dark suit, blameless. Then he turned down Bourbon directly into that gaudy crowd of humanity, his polite, unobtrusive figure casting among it something of dignity. With his hands in his pockets and his collar turned up against the rain, my beloved Claude receded—and disappeared for years.

$\mathcal{V}$oices of the $\mathcal{S}$outh

Lightning Source UK Ltd.
Milton Keynes UK
UKHW020938201122
412472UK00029B/450